THE OSHAWA PROJECT

1945: the War is over. A secret meeting takes place in Oshawa, Ontario between two powerful players in the post-war US Army, Donald Rogers and Mike Rafferty. The fragile alliance between the USA and the Soviets is being threatened by the aggressive outspokenness of one man — Brigadier General George Campion. Rogers enlists Rafferty into plotting Campion's expert assassination, to be funded by the German Reichsbank's abandoned gold reserves. Rafferty accepts reluctantly. But even a war hero can outlive his usefulness . . .

FREDERICK NOLAN

THE OSHAWA PROJECT

Complete and Unabridged

LINFORD
Leicester

First published in Great Britain

First Linford Edition
published 2007

British Library CIP Data

Nolan, Frederick W., *1931 –*
    The Oshawa Project.—Large print ed.—
Linford mystery library
    1. United States. Army—General staff
officers—Political activity—Fiction
    2. Conspiracy—Fiction
    3. Assassination—Fiction
    4. Detective and mystery stories
    5. Large type books
    I. Title
    823.9'14 [F]

ISBN 978–1–84617–836–8

Published by
F. A. Thorpe (Publishing)
Anstey, Leicestershire

Set by Words & Graphics Ltd.
Anstey, Leicestershire
Printed and bound in Great Britain by
T. J. International Ltd., Padstow, Cornwall

This book is printed on acid-free paper

In writing this book I had sterling assistance from some of the finest writers in the business. Let me particularly thank Ladislas Farago, Bickham Sweet-Escott, Peter Maas, Bruce Page, David Leitch, Phillip Knightley, Patrick Seale, Maureen McConville, Charles Whiting, Roger Manvell, Ian V. Hogg, Brian Ford and Kim Philby. If they hadn't written their books, there would have been no way I could have written mine.

1

Berlin
14 May 1945

By the time the speeches started, the General was drunk. He didn't act drunk, no slurring of his speech, no lurching about, none of that. But anyone who knew him well — and every correspondent at the press table knew Brigadier-General Robinson Campion Jr very well indeed — could see the signs. The bull-like swelling of the neck muscles, the lowering of the heavy eyebrows over glaring blue eyes, the almost-audible muttering, all these were signs as clear to those who knew Campion as are the symptoms of measles to a baby-doctor. And when General Campion was drunk, all hell was liable to break loose. So they watched him, and no one else. There had been a joint review that day. Every regiment in the Allied armies wanted to march at least one detachment through the shattered streets of Berlin, and the Supreme Commander was doing his best to accomodate them. The brass turned out in large numbers to sit on the reviewing stand, and usually some worthy nonentity whom his superiors wanted to pat on the back took the salute and made a speech at the dinner in the evening at American HQ. Today, there had also been a number of Russian generals at the parade, and they had obviously recognised Campion. He was easy enough to spot: that tightly-tailored combat jacket with its four rows of medal ribbons, the five overseas bars on the left sleeve topped by four chevrons from the earlier war, the bright shoulder patch of the 9th Army, the almost-pink gaberdine riding britches tucked into brilliantly-polished riding boots and, of course, the now-legendary Cavalry belt with its twin holsters, a silver-plated Colt's Frontier .45 on the right and a Smith & Wesson .375 Magnum on the left, the highly-polished helmet with its three stars, made Campion conspicuous even in as big a display of brass as this; and the Russians had been anxious to be friendly. Campion had given them what the correspondents called his 'War Face No. 5' — an expression he reserved for staff or civilians who had displeased him — discouraging their friendly overtures with a brusqueness that was tantamount to rudeness. But they had not been put off by Campion's bad manners and even now, in the big hall where the dinner was being held, they kept smiling and raising their glasses to him. And the more they did so, the more Campion drank, muttering into his glass.

Everywhere the eye moved there was brass. The tables were set out like an 'E' with the big 'names' on the top table, the spine of the 'E'. Oak leaves and stars, medals and ribbons everywhere. Loud male laughter and cigar smoke and the bluff, uneasy cameraderie of soldiers who do not speak well the language of their ally, mingled with the sense of pointless protocol and near-boredom caused by the knowledge that the war was over and you weren't quite used to it yet. These dinners were thrown because the upper echelons seemed to think it a good idea to 'cement relations' between the 'victorious Allies', but every one of the newsmen — who were always invited, and always came because the food and drink were considerably better than anything you could get anywhere else in Germany — knew it would take more than a few dinners with or without speeches to sort out the chaos that was coming. Roosevelt, Churchill and Stalin had drawn new lines for Europe the preceding February, and just working out the quadripartite division of Berlin was giving the brass headaches, let alone the thought of what Uncle Joe was going to do with all the bits of Eastern Europe he'd been handed on a plate. Most of the correspondents knew that Campion didn't think very much of the Yalta agreements, which he'd referred to (off the record, you guys) as a sell-out. He thought even less of the Russians, and had even been heard to say once or twice that America ought to have gone straight on past Berlin to Moscow while she had the army and the guns, because sooner or later America was going to have to fight the goddam Reds anyway. So they watched Campion slosh more brandy (from Goering's personal cellar) into his glass, watched the thin line of perspiration forming on the upper lip of Campion's personal aide, Lieutenant Colonel James Hansell French, watched the uneasy looks the British officer on Campion's right was giving him, and waited. They were not a cynical group of men, but the war was over, and a story was a story these days: anything Campion did was likely to be good copy.

Jim French sat tensely in his chair, his wine untouched in front of him, watching the press corps watching Campion. He had already been outside, and had briefed Campion's driver, Master Sergeant Bob Howard, to be ready to leave fast if he tipped him the signal. Howard was standing near the door and French looked his way. Howard gave him a slow nod: at least that was organised, thank God. French was not given to praying much: after five years of seeing his friends and enemies killed with totally impartial and random abandon, he had gotten out of the habit. But tonight he was praying silently that the General wouldn't blow his cork. French had seen the Supreme Commander taking strips off Campion's hide for shooting off his mouth in the wrong place at the wrong time to the wrong people and he didn't want to see it again. Campion was in bad *shtuck* with Eisenhower as it was, and another diplomatic gaffe would mean there'd be hell to pay. With the war over, everything had moved into the realm of 'politics', and Campion in a political situation was like a skunk at a picnic.

The Major-General from Eisenhower's staff got to his feet and tapped on his glass with a knife, calling for order. The throb of voices gradually quietened down to a subdued hum as he called upon the British General sitting at the centre of the top table to speak. There was a round of applause, with some hoarse cheers from the British contingent, as General Sir Anthony Sharp rose to his feet, shuffled his notes, and began to speak of great efforts and stirring deeds, men at arms and partners in war, his flat, nasal English accent becoming a drone in French's ears as he watched Campion. The General was glowering in earnest now, his big head swinging from left to right for all the world like some taunted fighting bull seeking its *querencia*, the small eyes peering belligerently from beneath the knitted brows as if seeking something to attack. Campion said something to the British officer on his left and French saw the man's head come up, distaste and offence written clearly on his horsey face. Oh, Christ, French thought wearily. His eyes moved to the press table, where the correspondents were making the pretence of taking notes on the British General's speech. At the corner of the table he could see Bill Mauldin scribbling on his sketchpad, and cursed silently. Campion hated Mauldin's dirty dogfaces, and had once gone clear to Supreme Headquarters to try to get orders issued that would make Mauldin draw cartoons with soldiers who looked, as Campion had put it, 'like American fighting men instead of two sonofabitching tramps.' Eisenhower had laughed Campion out of SHAEF, which had decidedly not made Campion's day and had assured Mauldin of the number one position on the General's shitlist. Mauldin had retaliated to Campion's attempt to pull rank by doing a wicked cartoon in which he had Willie and Joe saying; 'Yeah, I know, Willie, his guts and our blood' — a direct reference to Campion's legendary nickname. Keep your head down, Bill, French thought fervently.

General Sharp was droning on, talking about the spirit of mutual co-operation and finishing the Great Crusade in the Pacific. French switched him off again; his expertise in listening to speeches made by generals told him that General Sharp had some way to go yet. Get on with it, you old prick, he thought, feeling like one of those women in the movie serials, tied to the railway lines with the train coming hell-for-leather down the track and no help in sight. Campion was still pouring formidable shots of brandy into his glass and swigging them down like so much water. French shook his head. The man was incredible, all soldier.

He was unquestionably a hero, a heroic man. Yet he was drastically unpopular at the top. Although he had led the assaults on North Africa and Sicily, although he had won the admiration of the world with his breathtaking thrusts deep into the heart of the Third Reich, and although no soldier in the United States Army had better mastery of the military arts and sciences, Campion was considered by the people who made the ultimate decisions to be a royal pain in the ass, a monumental bore and a troublemaker who, while indispensable in wartime, was, now that the war was over, rapidly becoming a terrifying liability.

French heard General Sharp's voice take on a more decisive tone, rising to the theme of great leaders, sadly missed friends no longer with us to share the victor's crown, better times ahead for all mankind. Thank God, French thought, he's finishing. He was not alone in his thought, although others had perhaps different reasons. The hum of boredom in the air was palpable, and French could see that several members of the press contingent were openly talking among themselves, ignoring the speech completely.

'And so, as we look ahead to a bright tomorrow,' the British General said, raising his voice perhaps a quarter of an octave to compete with the buzz of whispering that was anticipating the end of his speech, 'I give you a toast! To those resilient, determined fighting men who met the Nazi horde in open battle and threw them back, broken, from the borders of their homeland! Gentlemen — the Russian Army!'

He raised his glass, and everyone in the room got to his feet, clinking his glass with his neighbour and murmuring the response to the toast. The translators told the Russian officers what had been said, and they beamed all over their faces, jumping to their feet and smacking their glasses against General Sharp's, nodding and smiling towards the crowded tables in front of them. Through the forest of raised arms and smiling faces turned towards the top table, French caught sight of Campion and groaned aloud.

Campion was sitting in his chair as if defying anyone to get him out of it. French left his chair and waved an arm at MS Howard, the signal to get the General's car to the door and keep the engine running. He moved carefully around the table and up behind his commanding officer, but before he could actually get next to Campion, he saw the British officer on Campion's left bend down and speak to him.

'Won't you drink the health of our Russian allies, sir?' he said.

'Not goddamned likely!' Campion barked, and the tone of voice he used cut through the babble of noise in the hall, stilling voices, stopping people in mid-movement, all heads turning towards the top table in a vacuum of silence into which Campion's next words fell like stones.

'Tell those Russian sonsofbitches that I'd sooner cut my goddamned throat than drink their health. Tell them I expect to have to go to war with them before I'm much older, and I'm damned if I'll drink with anyone I expect to have to fight.'

The silence was awful. French tried to move inconspicuously to Campion's side, but he was afraid to break the tension of the moment, feeling certain that pandemonium would ensue. The interpreter to whom Campion had spoken paled and looked from left to right, hoping for aid. None came.

'Tell him, goddammit!' roared Campion. 'That's an order, soldier!'

'General,' the British officer said, laying a hand on Campion's arm.

Campion brushed the man aside as if he were a fly, getting to his feet, towering over the others and glaring at the Russians as the interpreter whispered into the ear of the senior officer, a Colonel General whose barrel chest was completely covered with grandiose medals and stars. The man's eyes widened, and for perhaps two heartbeats he and Campion glared at each other, and then the Russian slapped the table hard with the flat of his hand and said something in Russian to the interpreter. The soldier nodded and then, coming to attention, said to Campion.

'Sir, the Colonel General says he feels exactly the same way about you, so won't you take a drink anyway?'

His words carried clearly, and everyone heard them. French saw one of the newspapermen fiddling with the flash equipment for his camera and the others getting to their feet, ready to come up fast, but before anyone else could move Campion burst out laughing, and after a second the Russian Colonel General started to laugh. Their laughter let the tension out of the scene as if someone had pulled a plug, and everyone started to roar with laughter, although French could feel the strain behind the pretended merriment, the sound just that shade louder, just that shade more forced than normal. He heard one of the press boys say, 'Christ, I thought that was going to be the start of World War Three!' Me too, brother, he thought, and got around behind Campion.

'Begging the General's pardon,' he said without inflection, 'but the General's car is outside.'

Campion looked up and glared at him,

but French didn't back off.

'It's eleven thirty, sir,' he said.

Campion nodded once, abruptly, then nodded again. He knew what French was doing and he knew why he was doing it. Just for a moment the piggy blue eyes narrowed as Campion debated whether or not to make an issue out of it, and then common sense prevailed. French felt a trickle of sweat run down his back inside his shirt. Campion nodded again, pushing back his chair. He swayed slightly and then his chin came up. He tugged the combat jacket down to its precise sit, and cleared his throat.

'With the General's permission,' he said. 'I've got a heavy day tomorrow.'

General Sharp nodded shortly, his narrow face showing his extreme displeasure. There was no doubt he was pleased to see Campion leaving, but the Russians, divining what was happening, got to their feet and clustered around the American, thrusting glasses with drinks in them towards him, wanting Campion to stay. The more they pressed, the tighter the thin line of Campion's lips grew. He pushed roughly through their ranks, French easing him along the line, shaking hands with one or two of the officers he knew, trying to get Campion to the exit. Campion was starting to mutter, quietly at first, then louder. He shook off the retaining hand that one of the Russian officers laid on his arm. 'Get your peasant paws off my uniform, you Baluchistan sheep-fucker,' he growled, tossing the man's hand aside as French rolled his eyes heavenward and prayed that none of the Russians understood Anglo-Saxon. The correspondents had stampeded around the tables to get to the door before Campion, and there was a lot of shouting, flashbulbs popping now, and the sound of outraged conversation in the big room forming a surging background to the scene. The newsmen formed a semi-circle in front of Campion that ebbed back as he thrust forward with his head down, French in front of him pushing the milling crowd back.

'Get out of my way, you shit-shovellers!' Campion shouted, 'Get back!'

'Come on, General,' someone shouted.

'Give us a quote.'

Campion stopped dead in his tracks, his hands on his hips not too far from the silver-plated pistols in their holsters. The pressmen fell back, almost cowering. There was a well-founded rumour that Campion had once pulled those guns on an interviewer and threatened to adapt his undercarriage if he asked any more personal questions.

'Quote?' he growled. 'You want a quote? By God, I'll give you one!'

'General,' French said, warningly, 'This way, General.'

'One minute, mister!' Campion said. 'Take this down,' he went on, his index finger transfixing the correspondents in front of him. 'You can tell anyone who wants to hear it that General George Campion says he does not believe the future of half of the world can be left in the hands of Mongol bootmakers and Siberian potato farmers. If we don't fight the bastards now, we're — '

French stood on ceremony no longer. He barged into Campion from behind, pushing the bigger man forward, moving him towards the door as MS Howard came in with three MP's, forming a sort of flying wedge with Campion in its centre and French at the rear, Campion bellowing back over his shoulder as they bum's-rushed him for the door, the reporters scrambling up on chairs, desks, trying to get a good photo of the incredible scene, flashbulbs popping everywhere, crunching underfoot as they got Campion out into the street and across the pavement to the car standing with its doors wide open.

'Time somebody spoke up!' Campion yelled defiantly as they bundled him any whichway into the back of the car. French fell in after his superior officer, almost taking the fingers off the hand of one of the reporters as he slammed the door and yelled, 'Get the hell out of here!' to the driver. Howard let in the clutch with a jerk that threw Campion and French into a sprawling heap as they rocketed away from the kerb, the newspapermen scattering out of the staff car's path, still trying for photographs as the car roared off down the street. French looked out of the tinted rear window, saw the MP's herding the pressmen off the pavement, and then relaxed, leaning back against the cushions, his face streaming with sweat. Campion was sitting bolt upright, a look of intense yet satisfied anger on his face. He knew what he had done and he was glad.

'*Jesus*, General,' French said.

2

Oshawa
23 May 1945

The big white rambling building set amid close-growing pine and birch on the shores of Lake Ontario looked like a rich city-dweller's ideal of what a farmhouse should look like. It stood on a low bluff that provided its occupants with a superb view over the wind-stippled expanse of the lake and the chugging ferries shuttling between Toronto and Rochester. Although by now the outbuildings and sheds scattered throughout the cleared spaces in the trees bore only the most passing of resemblances to barns or stables, there were still enough white fences, still enough carefully rough stone paths to give the place a countryfied air entirely out of keeping with its actual purpose and to preserve the illusion that it was what it had once been and would soon be again, the country home of a millionaire with a passion for privacy.

The house was far enough out of town to ensure that the local people spent little time wondering about the high electrified fence or the huge man in the dark suit who guarded the gate at the main entrance. After all, the owner was one of those high muckymuck British diplomats, and if from time to time someone in town remarked on the constant coming and going of young, tough-looking men (and sometimes women) up at the big house, well, there was a war on. They figured it probably had something to do with the war effort, so they were for it. The townspeople were glad enough of the business they got from Sir William, and he was a prompt payer for the sometimes surprising quantities of food and drink and household goods he seemed to need. Some of them, of course, made guesses as to the true function of the house on the hill. None of them ever really came close to the truth, which was that the country residence of Sir William Stephenson was the training school for operatives of the

American OSS and the British SOE. In the past five years every agent of both organisations had received part, if not all, of his training in Oshawa.

Both the men sitting now in the library of the north wing had been trained here, and knew each other well. On the table in front of them were yellow ruled legal pads, an Anglepoise lamp, a bottle of Dimple Haig and an ashtray already over-flowing with butts. Both were in casual weekend clothes.

'It's a hell of a proposition, Don,' the one nearest the window said. He was about thirty, his fair hair just beginning to recede from his forehead. His blue eyes were alert and lively although his face was thin and foxy, the mouth weak. The man sitting opposite him was also thin, but tougher, mean-looking. Affecting heavy horn-rimmed spectacles he did not need, his skin had that faint tinge of olive that hints at Mediterranean forebears. His name was Donald Rogers and he was Senior Executive Officer in the Operations Division of SHAEF — the Supreme Headquarters of the American forces in Europe — in

Frankfurt. His job there was, simply put, to make the day-to-day running of the monstrous machine which had grown out of the greatest army ever seen on the face of the earth as painless and as simple as possible for the Supreme Commander, General Dwight D. Eisenhower. Together with Ike's other Exec, Walt Gilchriese, Rogers pretty well controlled the monster. The two of them were known, not affectionately, as 'Mutt and Jeff,' and if Gilchriese perhaps inspired grudging respect, Rogers reduced many — and these included visiting Senators, Congressmen and other species of top brass — to something close to abject fear, the result of which was that pretty well everyone hated his guts. It didn't seem to bother him overmuch. One of his more famous quotes was, 'Every man at the top needs a sonofabitch to look out for him, and I'm Ike's.' Next to Eisenhower himself, Rogers was the hardest man to see in Frankfurt, and you had to see Rogers before you could see Eisenhower. Rafferty knew what they said about Rogers in Washington: beneath the tip of the iceberg is the iceberg. Deep down, they said, he's deep. Beneath that shitty exterior is a shitty interior. And so on. Rogers quite obviously thrived on it. He set internal policies at SHAEF with Gilchriese, their power extending clear to the top in every branch of military government in Europe. Neither man was a soldier in the conventional sense, but their power, in relation to their normal rank of Colonel US Army, was enormous. And Rafferty knew better than to argue too much against it. Within certain areas, Rogers could do just exactly what he damned well wanted to do. Rafferty thought, reflecting upon the limited power he himself had as Assistant Commander, European Sector, in the Office of Strategic Services, Washington, even with the same military rank as Rogers.

Their meeting at Oshawa was clandestine, although no one would have thought to question it anyway. Rafferty had *laissez-passer* throughout OSS. Both men had concurred that the 'psychological distance' between this secluded place and

Washington was a wise choice of venue for their meeting. Washington gossip was viciously thorough and generally accurate. They could do without it.

'A hell of a proposition,' Rafferty repeated.

'I know that,' Rogers said testily. 'But think, man, *think*. Ike has already let it be known that he has political ambitions. He'll be the biggest conquering hero you've ever seen when he comes back to the States. He'll walk any nomination — and at a guess I'd say he'll be nominated in 'fifty-two as sure as hens lay eggs — and waltz into the White House without even having to put up a fight. He's going to be the next President of the United States, Mike, and when he is, I intend to be there, or thereabouts, getting mine. And I'll want people who've helped out, people like you, on my team.'

'Yes,' Rafferty said, unable not to be pleased by Rogers' words, 'but this . . . '

'Dammit, man,' Rogers snapped. 'You weren't so coy when we took our chances over the Merkers project. You've got your piece of the Trust — a nice, steady hundred thousand a year. Don't you want more?' Before Rafferty could answer, he went on, pushing the man harder. 'Listen, you know Truman's going to disband OSS in the fall. You must do, everyone's talking about it. What will you get when they toss you out on to the street? An army pension? A Good Conduct Medal? A written letter from the President? Shit, Rafferty, if that's all you want . . . '

'No, Don,' Rafferty said, his voice tentative. 'You know I want — well, I mean, with the Trust paying out every year, I can take it easy. You know, no problems.'

'Sure,' Rogers said, 'You don't want to play with the big boys.'

'Oh, yes,' Rafferty protested. 'Yes, I do. But — Don, are you sure this is what — what Ike wants?'

'You mean did he come up to me at HQ and say, 'Don, do me a favour, knock off that bastard Campion for me, okay?' No, he didn't.'

'Then how can you be sure?'

'The way he is, the things he says whenever Campion's name comes up.

Jesus, Ike is so screwed up over that loudmouthed bastard you wouldn't believe it. You know, Ike's very conscious of having been made Supremo way over the heads of a lot of men who were his seniors. That's why he leans over backwards to avoid pulling rank on them. Goddammit, he's had enough reasons to bust Campion ten times in the last six months alone. Look.' He raised his hand and ticked off fingers as he made his points. 'One, Campion got his name dragged through the mud when those two officers were tried for shooting POWs and as much as said Campion had given them the OK by his example. Ike bailed him out. He bailed him out again after that speech in England.'

'You mean the one in Yorkshire?'

'Leeds, right. He only said' — there was a world of scorn in the way Rogers used the word 'only' — 'that it was the manifest destiny of the British and Americans to rule the postwar world. Not a goddamn word about the Russians, nothing. Jesus, the headlines!'

'I remember,' Rafferty said.

'I tell you, Mike, if Ike had had Campion in front of him the day that story broke, he'd have shot his balls off personally. But what happens? He bails him out again.'

'Why?'

'I don't know, and that's the truth. When we were in combat, I could figure it: expediency — he needed the General and so he put up with the mouth. Now . . . well, maybe our judgement is right, he's soft on coming down on his nominal superiors. He's never really gotten used to how fast and how far he climbed. He keeps on telling himself he's got to be more cold-blooded, but when push comes to shove, he can't cut the mustard. Which is where I come in.'

Rafferty nodded. Rogers' reputation as Eisenhower's hatchetman was such that news of an impending visit by him had been known to reduce fighting generals to quivering wrecks. There had been occasions when Rogers had used the executive powers his job gave him both unsparingly and devastatingly.

'Even so, Don, that's not enough

reason for him to want Campion taken out — permanently.'

'I'm not through giving you reasons,' Rogers said coldly. 'Did you know that just before Leclerc took Paris, Campion accused Ike of freezing him out of the glory?'

'No!'

'Well he not only did it, but he did it in front of a crowd of British brass. Crazy as a bedbug. Only last week he rang up Ike's deputy . . . '

'Joe McNarney?'

'General Joe himself, and told him on the telephone — on the phone, mind you, and to hell with who might be listening in — that we ought to recruit any Germans who've had military training into the US Army right now, and take out after the Russians before they have a chance to recover from the war. Said we'll have to fight the Russkies sooner or later anyway, so it might as well be while we're strong.'

'Christ,' Rafferty said feelingly. 'He must really have popped his cork.'

'Oh, I don't know,' Rogers said; then: 'He's crazy like a fox, that one. He's already in for Stateside leave. He'll be over here next month, you'll see, sashaying around like Jesse James with those fucking sixguns strapped on, leading parades, getting the freedom of the city of Knee Jerk, Tennessee, profiling for the newsreels — America's idea of a fighting man, Old Bloodyguts Campion.' He paused for a moment, lighting a cigarette. 'He knows he's in trouble, Mike. He's putting up a front, daring Ike to cut him down after the hero's welcome.'

'And will he?'

'He can't. Crazy like a fox, see?'

'Ship him out.'

'That's been tried. In fact, Campion wants out himself. He's going to ask the Secretary of War for reassignment to the Far East. He isn't going to get it, according to our information.'

'So?'

'Back to Bavaria, back into our laps. Our problem. Which is why those of us who've seen this building up are convinced we have to act. If Campion is allowed to go on shooting off his mouth about the United States going to war with Russia, we're going to have the mother-fuckingest confrontation in Germany the world has ever seen. But if Ike is presented with a *fait accompli*, he won't kick, and I think I can guarantee nobody would dig into it too much. It will have just been — handled. Later on, when things are settled — about the future I mean — we'll be in. Like that.'

He extended his hand with the index and second fingers crossed. Rafferty nodded, getting up from the table and pacing in front of the open stone fireplace. Rogers said nothing. Rafferty went across to the bar in the corner of the room and built himself a drink.

'All right,' he said. 'Supposing.'

Rogers leaned forward intently as Rafferty came back to the table and sat down. His glass made a wet ring on the polished surface and he wiped it with a handkerchief.

'Supposing I agree,' Rafferty said, running his fingers around the rim of the glass, staring down, frowning slightly. 'It's going to be very tough to organise.'

'Agreed,' Rogers said. 'That's why I came to you, Mike.'

'How about money?'

Rogers nodded, a slow smile touching his lips.

'Mike, when we set up the Merkers project in May, we had nothing. Just an organisation that could be — used. There were — well, a lot of people involved. Everyone who contributed got a pension, like yours. The Trust. Well, there's plenty of money from the same source, if we need it. Plenty.'

'Okay.'

It had been an astonishing undertaking, and Rafferty had only been on the fringes. He had provided certain information about security to Rogers, without at that time knowing exactly what it was for. It was only two months later that he understood, and then, of course, he was in up to his eyes. The 385th Infantry had stumbled on an abandoned industrial saltmine at Merkers. Down the shafts they found the entire German Reichsbank gold reserves, together with assorted art treasures and other valuables, including a wooden crate full of gold fillings from teeth, presumably from the concentration camps. The gold alone was worth more than $250,000,000. It had completely disappeared in transit to the vaults at Frankfurt. The most intensive investigation had not turned up any clues. The file was still open. That was what Rogers now called the Merkers project. The Trust Rafferty knew nothing about, except that it paid each quarter the sum of $25,000 into a bank account he had opened with Wells Fargo in San Francisco.

'How much do you estimate you might need?'

'A hundred thousand, maybe. Not more.'

'You've got it.'

'Right,' Rafferty said. 'Conditions?'

'Some,' Rogers said. 'It's got to be done with no comeback, Mike. That means some kind of accident. No Tommy guns, knifings, no cheap hood tricks like dynamite wired to the ignition key. What we're looking for here is an accident, a tragic accident.'

His grin was satanic, and if Rafferty

had looked closer, he might have seen a faint hint of triumph in Rogers' expression, too, but he didn't.

'So, we need a total concept,' Rafferty said, running his hand through his thinning, sandy hair. 'Something unlike anything we've handled before.'

'You say,' Rogers said.

'We can't use a team,' Rafferty went on, ignoring Rogers' ironic comment on OSS methods, 'because there's too much likelihood of a leak. We can't use anyone known to any security agency, for the same reasons. That tends to narrow the options a little.'

He smiled at his own understatement.

'But you have some ideas?'

'Some,' Rafferty replied. 'It'll take a little travelling time, and I'll have to swing close, but things are fairly easy right now, end of the war, nobody checking anything too much. With OSS up for disbandment, and Donovan being touted for an ambassadorship someplace, everyone's got that 'it won't be long now' feeling. Yes, I reckon I can swing it. But we'll have to go outside, there's no alternative.'

'I follow your reasoning, but isn't that dangerous?'

'Not if it's played right.'

'For instance?'

'There's a man called Luciano,' Rafferty said softly.

'Luciano? You mean . . . ?'

'Yes, that Luciano,' Rafferty said. 'There was talk 'way back in '43 that he fixed things in Sicily for the Third Army. I don't know the details. But I do know he's helped the Navy on a quid pro quo basis. The boys at Church Street in New York had troubles in the harbour: word kept getting out to the U-Boats about sailing dates, cargoes. They were picking ships off like fish in a barrel. The Navy went to Luciano up in Dannemora. He gave them it with a pink ribbon tied around it: the whole New York waterfront, closed down, not a word, *shtumm*.'

'What was the deal?'

'Something quite simple, really. They moved him out of Dannemora — that's a maximum security pen — and down to Albany, a 'trusty' prison called Great Meadows. Free access to his lawyer. All the visitors he wanted. Things like that. He runs his rackets from up there, I guess.'

'And what can we offer him?'

'A favour for a favour. I'll tell him OSS needs a favour. If he plays, OSS will put in a good word when his parole comes up, say he's rendered us valuable service and we'd like it taken into account.'

'I don't like that,' Rogers said. 'You tell him you're OSS, and there's a way back to you. And then to us.'

'No way at all,' Rafferty said. 'I use a false ID — no problem, I can get one in ten minutes on my own authority. By the time Luciano's parole comes up, there won't be any OSS.'

'We don't want to cross him up,' Rogers said. 'He's connected to some other people we know, remember.'

'No cross-up,' Rafferty insisted. 'Shit, we didn't know OSS was going to be disbanded, did we?'

Rogers grinned. This was his kind of meat and he liked the way Rafferty's mind was working. Besides, he had another reason for being sure that

Luciano would never believe he had been crossed up, but he wasn't about to mention it to Rafferty.

'Okay, will Luciano go for it?'

'Tell me why he wouldn't.'

'No play. Go on.'

'All we want from him is a name. That's all. He's got connections in Italy, all over. He puts us on to a pro, a top pro, in Europe. I go to Europe and hire him, using the same alias I use for Luciano. Right so far?'

'One thousand percent.'

'Questions.'

'I think I'll take that drink now,' Rogers said, getting up slowly from the table, stretching his arms above his head. 'Another for you?'

'Yeah, Scotch and water.'

Rogers poured the drinks, taking his time. He came back to the table and put the drinks down.

'What about the pro, the man who does the job? If he's got a connection with the Mafia, they've got a connection with us. Can it lead back?'

'No. If he is a pro, he doesn't ask

questions. We've been sent by someone. That's all. He gets paid, does his job, and gets lost. No comeback. They're very hard on people who try to blackmail them.'

'And the contact Luciano gives you?'

'He'll have the same name, the same alias as everyone else. He won't know me from Adam's off ox.'

'Good,' Rogers said. 'Then we're in business.' He held up his glass and watched Rafferty's face. Now was the big moment. He saw the expression and said *Goddamn* silently inside himself.

'Qualms, Mike?' he asked softly.

'Not qualms, exactly. But . . . '

'Then listen to me,' Rogers said, his voice hypnotic now and commanding.

'The reason I'm talking to you is because I know you can do this, Mike, and do it well. You're one of the best people on the team, and nobody's going to forget that when shareout time comes. The fact is, Mike, we tried it without the kind of expertise that only someone like you can provide, and it damned near blew up in our faces.'

Rafferty sat there, just looking, just

listening. Good, Rogers told himself, good. Just keep listening now, baby.

'Nobody's heard about this over here, yet,' he went on. 'It's top-top secret and you know why it is. But I'll tell you some of it. Last month Campion was flying to 25th Corps HQ at Bielefeld. En route, the Piper Cub he was travelling in was attacked by a Spitfire — no, wait, hear me out — a Spitfire. Christ knows how that Cub stayed in the air, but it did. Campion should have been shot to ribbons but he stepped out at Bielefeld without a scratch. There was a godawful stink. They found out that the Spitfire had been flown by a Polish pilot named Wysowski who claimed he'd screwed up his navigation and thought Campion's plane was a German staff transport.'

'But that's — ' Rafferty burst out.

'Hard to believe, I know,' Rogers said grimly. 'But it happened. It was all hushed up by . . . someone. The pilot seems to have disappeared. Anyway. The point of the story is this. When we told the Old Man about it, he said in many ways it had been a pity that the Pole hadn't been a German, and succeeded in shooting Campion down. He said that what he wished for Campion more than anything else was a hero's death.'

'He said that?'

'So, as they say, I am reliably informed.'

He drained his glass and put it down firmly on the table, holding on to it and looking at Rafferty. This was it. He could hear a clock ticking somewhere.

'Okay,' Rafferty said. 'I'm in.'

'Good,' Rogers said. 'One last thing, Mike. He has to be taken out before Christmas.'

'Can do.'

Rogers stood up and extended his hand. They shook, gravely, sealing a pact.

'One for the road,' Rogers said, and Rafferty nodded. He watched Rogers go across to the bar, a lean, compact, buttoned-down man who held his life in the palm of his hand. Funny, he didn't even like Rogers. He took the drink and raised it in a gesture of salute.

'Look at it another way,' Rogers said, finishing the drink and getting into his overcoat. 'The old fucker's outlived his usefulness anyway.'

Rafferty drank his whisky fast, to settle the angry bile that rose in his throat. There was no reason for him to hate Rogers, yet suddenly he did. He wasn't ready yet to face the truth about who he really hated.

3

Great Meadows
30 May 1945

'Charlie, this is Major James Lawrence, from Washington.'

Rafferty nodded at the man who got up from the sofa in the Warden's office to shake his hand. Luciano — or to give him his correct name Lucania — was in good shape for a man who had spent the last twenty years inside. His skin had a healthy glow with no trace of prison pallor, the heavy-lidded eyes were sharp and clear. He was wearing a tan cashmere sweater with a pale-yellow open-necked shirt under it, off-white chino pants. His belt and shoes were of matching black crocodile leather.

'Major,' Luciano said, letting a thin grin touch his wide, thick lips.

'What outfit you with, Jimmy, Army or Navy?'

'Neither,' Rafferty said shortly. 'I'm in intelligence.'

Luciano's eyes darted swiftly left, looking toward his lawyer, whose bland face revealed absolutely nothing. Moses Polakoff was one of the top criminal lawyers in New York, and the mobsters held him in the highest respect first because he had been successful in getting many of them released or acquitted over the last decade or so, and second because he had the reputation of keeping his mouth shut. Even though Luciano had finally gone down before the intense onslaught launched against him by the crusading Tow Dewey, pulling a thirty-to-fifty at Dannemora, Luciano respected the lawyer and still retained him, leaning heavily these days upon his shrewd business judgement.

'Major Lawrence is okay, Charlie,' Polakoff said in his well-modulated voice. 'I've seen his credentials. He's with intelligence, like he says.'

'You ever hear of OSS, Mr Luciano?' Rafferty said. Luciano smiled and nodded. They sat down, Polakoff in the Warden's desk chair, Luciano back on his sofa, and Rafferty in the armchair in front of the desk. Polakoff had asked the Warden if they could talk alone. Rafferty had been surprised, even though he had expected it, to see how readily the Warden had concurred.

'It's a matter of getting some advice, Mr Luciano,' he said.

'Sure,' Luciano replied, grinning like a snake. 'What kind of advice?'

Rafferty told him the story he had concocted. There was a long silence after he finished talking. Then Luciano slapped his thigh and laughed out loud, his head thrown back, showing the gold fillings in his teeth.

'Jeeeezus!' he chuckled. 'This I don't believe. The US Government is goin' into the rackets now?'

'Charlie,' Polakoff said softly. 'Hear him out.'

'Sorry, sorry, Counsellor, sorry, Major,' Luciano said, still grinning. 'Go on, go on.'

'I need a top pro, Mr Luciano,' Rafferty said. 'The very best.'

'What you got in mind, kid? A gun? Explosives? Knives? What?'

'It's got to be rigged. An accident,' Rafferty said. 'I'm afraid that's all I can tell you.'

'Shit, that's all right, kid. There's plenty of guys . . . '

'No,' Rafferty interrupted. 'Not an American. Someone in Europe.'

Luciano looked at his lawyer, a slight edginess showing in his eyes.

'Hey, what is this?' he said. 'What is this, Moses?'

'It's all right, Charlie,' the lawyer said.

Luciano nodded, sticking his full lower lip out reflectively.

'Yeah, yeah, okay,' he said. 'I got a couple of contacts in the old country. That the sort of thing you mean?'

'Yes,' Rafferty said, leaning forward, trying not to let his eagerness show.

'Italy,' Luciano said. 'I could give you a name, someone to talk to in Italy.'

'Fine,' Rafferty said. 'What's the name, and where do I find him?'

'Hey, hold on there, Jimmy,' Luciano said, leaning back and holding up a hand.

'First of all, what's in this for me? What're you offerin'?'

'You'll be up for parole come November, Mr Luciano,' Rafferty said. 'I checked. A good word from us would go a long way in your favour.'

Again the look from Luciano to the lawyer. Rafferty thought he detected a slight nod from the man in the Warden's chair. Luciano's face brightened.

'Okay, okay,' he said. 'That's kosher with me, Jimmy. I done a few favours already for the government, you know it? Now, them Navy boys, they got me moved over here from Dannemora. If you was to say you could get me moved out of here altogether . . . ?'

'No chance, Mr Luciano,' Rafferty said. 'You're here for the duration. Unless the parole board recommends otherwise. There I can do something.'

'Jesus,' Luciano said. 'I practically get the whole fuckin' Army through Sicily and what do I get? A big thank you. I fix it so the Navy don't get no more hassle on the docks. What do I get? Another big thank you. What the fuck you guys think I

45

am, some sort of charity or somethin'?'

'Charlie,' the lawyer began, but Luciano waved him silent.

'No, no, Moses,' he said. 'Leave this one to me, right?'

Polakoff shrugged. He had stayed in business with these people by knowing when to argue and when to shut up. He shut up.

'We'll make a deal, you an' me, Jimmy,' the mobster said. 'You guys ship three crates of seven-year-old Scotch up here, two, three cartons of butts — Chesterfields, okay? And I want a broad.'

Rafferty just looked at Luciano. Luciano leaned back and grinned unrepentantly, like a kid caught stealing cookies who knows his mother won't punish him.

'I can swing the liquor and the cigarettes,' Rafferty said finally. 'But no women, Mr Luciano. No way.'

Luciano bounded to his feet and grabbed Rafferty's hand, pumping it up and down.

'You got a deal, Jimmy,' he said. 'Hey, I never figured to get no broad in here, anyway. Although it'd sure as hell be somethin', wouldn't it? The boys'd never stop talkin' about it. You sure you can't do it?' He looked at Rafferty mischievously. Rafferty nodded. 'Sure,' he said.

'Ah, well,' Luciano said. 'I take your word for it, okay?' He turned to the lawyer. 'See, Moses? Told you to leave it to me.'

'That's right, Charlie,' Polakoff said heavily.

'The name, Mr Luciano,' Rafferty said.

'Lucky, Lucky,' Luciano insisted. 'Call me Lucky. Everybody does.'

'Lucky,' Rafferty said. 'How about that name?'

'Oh, sure,' Luciano said. 'His name's — ' he stopped, cocking a squinting eye at Rafferty. 'Hey, how I know you won't tip him to the Feds?'

'Why would I do that, Lucky?' Rafferty asked. 'I need him myself.'

'Yeah, I guess that's right,' Luciano said. 'Anyway, Moses says you're okay, which is kosher with me. You go to Naples, right? You see a guy named Tony Esposito. Moses will give you the address and a note saying you're okay. He'll help you out.'

'Tony Esposito,' Rafferty said. 'Thanks, Mr Lu . . . Lucky.'

'Don't mensh, don't mensh,' Luciano said. He was feeling expansive now that he had won his cheap victory over the booze and the cigarettes, Rafferty thought.

'Okay, is that all?' Luciano said, getting up. He looked cheerful, a man ahead of the game. Rafferty decided it was time to throw the curve ball.

'I want a meet with this Esposito set up for next week, Lucky.'

'Next week?' Luciano said blankly. He looked at Polakoff and then back at Rafferty. 'What's with you, Jimmy? You *pazzo*, or something? You think I got a phone in my cell, I can call long distance to Italy, set this up in ten minutes or somethin'?'

'As a matter of fact that's exactly what I do think, Lucky,' Rafferty said with a straight face. Luciano looked at him angrily for a moment and then his face fell apart. He roared with laughter, slapping Polakoff on the back.

'I like this one, Moses,' he said, chortling. 'He's got balls.'

'Yes, Charlie,' the lawyer said, moving away. Rafferty got the strange feeling that Polakoff did not care for the physical contact. He didn't feel one bit sorry for the man.

'Right,' Luciano said. 'You fix it so I get to a phone, call New York, okay. No bugs, no tapes, nothin', okay?'

Rafferty nodded. 'Okay,' he said.

'Good,' Luciano said. 'That's all there is to it, Jimmy. You leave it all to me, *capisce*? You'll get a call from the Counsellor here, two days from now — that's Friday, right?'

'Right,' Rafferty said.

'And Friday I expect a CARE parcel from you,' Luciano said. 'Or when you get to Napoli you get your peewee fed to the fishes, you know what I mean?'

'Just make the call,' Rafferty said. 'And save the hard talk for the punks on Tenth Avenue.'

Luciano shook his head admiringly.

'See, Moses,' he said. 'I told you he had balls. Listen, Jimmy, any time you want a job, you come and see me, you hear? I can always use a man who's got balls.'

'Thanks,' Rafferty said, smiling to take the sting out of his words. 'I'll keep it in mind in case my luck ever runs out.'

'Great, kid, great,' Luciano said, putting his hand on Rafferty's shoulder. He walked him across to the door, and banged on it with his fist. An armed guard came in with the Warden.

'Stick around, Moses,' Luciano said to his lawyer. 'I got to talk to you.'

'In your cell, though, Mr Luciano, if you please,' the Warden said. 'I have to do some work today.'

'Sure, sweetheart,' Luciano grinned, and patted the Warden's florid face with mock affection that brought the blood rushing to the man's face.

Rafferty saw his fist clench beneath the desk top, and Luciano saw it too. He burst out laughing, and he was still chuckling when the armed guard opened the door leading to the corridor which went across to the cells. Luciano went through the doorway ahead of his lawyer, tall and erect like some monarch walking through his palace. Rafferty heard one of the trusties sweeping the corridor call out

'Keep punchin', Lucky,' and saw Luciano wave a regal hand in acknowledgement. Then the closing door shut him from sight. Within ten minutes Rafferty was on his way back to New York.

4

He had no problem getting the time off. He was due more than a month's vacation, and when he suggested that he could use the time usefully by checking on one or two outstanding cases in Europe, his travel papers had been expedited by SHAEF with commendable speed. He had gotten a lift from the airport in the jeep of a young Navy lieutenant who was returning to his ship. He had told the driver to stop on the via Nova del Campo di Marte so that Rafferty could see the whole astonishing sweep of the bay below, Capri sharp and blue on the horizon. Vesuvius benign across to the southwest behind Barra. That night, the young lieutenant, whose name was Harwood Hinton and who came from New Mexico, had shown

Rafferty around the town.

There were new buildings rising every-where, arc lights blazing as the men worked through the night as though racing against time to create a new post-war world to live in. They ogled the spectacular whores in the Galleria Umberto who stood gossiping in the soft evening warmth, their bodies straining every seam of the tight silk dresses. In the Corso Umberto there were blind men making wastepaper baskets on the side-walks. American servicemen thronged the streets, many of them dead drunk, reeling riotously along, followed by chanting Italian children. They ate in a restaurant near the Galleria, and pathetic skinny youngsters, no more than seven or eight years old, sidled up to their table holding out their hands, eyes pathetic, saying '*diece lire, diece lire*'. When Rafferty finally gave in and handed them some coins, they winked and moved on to the next table, repeating the performance, consummate professionals. There were sidewalk vendors everywhere, even late at night, and the shill for the barrel organ that they stopped to listen to for a moment came up and asked for money. Hinton shook his head, waving the man away. 'Hokay, then, cigarette?' the man said. They walked up the via Santa Brigida and into the via Roma, where the whores were blatant and sometimes surprisingly beautiful, then down to the via Caracciola, looking southwest at the lights and the dark, oily beauty of the unseen bay. Lovers went by them in the darkness locked in tight embrace, and now and again a jeep roared along the sea front, its occupants singing loudly, waving bottles of Capri wine or cheap *grappa*.

Rafferty had a last drink with Hinton in the Piazza Municipio, the last port of call for the sailors lurching back to their ships in the harbour. He stood with Hinton on the pavement, looking across at the turrets of the old castle. It looked as if it belonged in the Loire valley. Two Navy MPs sitting in a jeep glared at them, as if daring them to start something.

After he said goodnight to Hinton, Rafferty walked back to his hotel on the via Sanfelice, feeling slightly drunk, slightly lonely. He ought not to have spent time with Hinton, he thought, but what the hell, Hinton would never remember him.

Everything had been laid on in advance, no problems, no questions asked. Rogers had a long arm, but Rafferty made a mental note to kid him next time he saw him about the fact that his hotel room looked out on the flat roof of an apartment building next door where the cats yowled all night and the ancient plumbing gurgled and choked in the myriad pipes that ran down the wall. Big time he thought, finally drifting into sleep, the flat attaché case with the money in it beneath his pillow. The tensions of the last weeks were eased by the balmy, almost fetid Neapolitan air. He awoke feeling good, and went downstairs. There was a message for him at the desk. It was short and simple: YOU WILL BE CALLED FOR AT ELEVEN, it said. He looked at his watch. He had time to go out and get some coffee, walk around for a while. The thought of eating breakfast was no longer attractive, and that aching tension in his gut was back.

An hour later he was in the back of an army jeep, its markings faded, bouncing up into the warren of alleys off the via Roma, going sharply uphill. The driver leaned on his horn the whole time, ambling pedestrians ignoring its blast and the chattering clash of the gears as the jeep roared by. He caught glimpses of naked children playing in a square called Piazza Concordia; on the shady side of a street fruit and vegetables were laid out for sale on barrows, on tables, with women poking around, shopping while the vendors chased away thieving kids who clustered around as persistent as the droning clouds of flies. Aimless men sat on doorsteps as if waiting for something, anything to happen, eyes closed, dozing in the warm sun. An elderly couple were playing cards in a room that opened directly on to the street, and inside another house he saw a dark-haired girl brushing her hair in front of a mirror, her naked breasts high and proud and olive-brown. He had no idea which way they had come or where they were. The driver turned around, grinning at Rafferty and displaying teeth that looked like Gorgonzola cheese.

'Stink here, no?' he said cheerfully.

'Watch the street, for Christ's sake!' Rafferty yelled as they narrowly missed two boys who came darting out of a side alley. The driver laughed aloud as if Rafferty had made a good joke, then gunned the motor, wheeling sharply around a corner and up a short steep hill, gunning the motor again as he made a right into a cool, shadowed courtyard. Someone Rafferty could not see closed gates behind them. The driver switched off the engine.

'*Ecco*,' he said, and pointed at a stairway across the courtyard. There was an unused fountain in the centre of the court, and on the far side an old truck was jacked up. Three men were standing, looking at the disassembled engine on the oil-smeared cobbles at their feet without a great deal of interest. There was a balcony running around the house at the first-floor level, and none-to-clean washing hung in drooping lines from one side to the other, right across the courtyard. Rafferty went up the rickety wooden staircase, and when he came on to the balcony, found a door directly opposite him. He knocked, wondering why he was nervous.

'*Pronto*,' a voice said.

Rafferty pushed the door open and went into the dark interior. It was a tiny room filled with a ragbag collection of broken-down furniture: sad-looking chairs, a sprung bed that sagged in the middle, its brass knobs tarnished. There was a man sitting on the bed. Rafferty could not see him clearly at first, but as his eyes became accustomed to the gloom, he realised that the seated man was totally out of place in these surroundings. He was wearing a light-weight gaberdine suit and a pale blue shirt that had to be silk. He looked cool and self-contained, and his long-jawed lantern face was expressionless. Rafferty could not see the man's eyes: they were shaded behind tinted lenses.

'Signor Esposito?' he said.

'That's me,' the man said. Brooklyn, by

God, or the Bronx, Rafferty thought.

'Lawrence,' he said. 'Mr . . . '

'I know who sent you, Mr Lawrence,' the man said. 'You want to let me see some kind of identification?'

Rafferty handed him the envelope with Luciano's note in it, and his ID card. The man scanned both carefully, looking up to compare Rafferty with his photograph.

'You was younger when this was took, right?'

'And I've had a lot of worries,' Rafferty said.

'Okay, Mr Lawrence,' the man said heavily. 'You made your point: you're a hard man an' you wanna talk business. Right?'

Rafferty said nothing.

'What you're askin' for, that's a tall order these days, you know it?' Esposito said. 'However, for a friend of Mister Lucky's . . . I think we can help you out.'

He reached behind him and lifted a slim leather briefcase on to his knees. Opening it, he took out a folder, Army issue. Esposito caught Rafferty's look and grinned.

'On'y place you can get decent stuff,' he said. 'In here are some instructions. A meet has been set up for you with a man known to, uh, me and my associates. His name is Shelley.'

'He's reliable?'

'We are vouching for him, Mr Lawrence,' Esposito said, and Rafferty thought he detected a note of injured pride in the man's voice.

He held his tongue, reaching forward for the folder in Esposito's hand. The man drew it away.

'There is the matter of our fee,' he said.

'Nobody said anything . . . ' Rafferty began angrily, but Esposito held up a hand.

'Two thousand dollars, Mr Lawrence,' he grinned, showing fine white teeth.

'Cash on the barrelhead.'

'This had better be on the level,' Rafferty said. 'If I ask . . . '

'Ask him,' Esposito said. 'He should know better than anyone what it's like out here. Listen, Lawrence,' he went on, jabbing a finger at the standing man. 'Out here, I run things, see? I do like Mister

Lucky wants because he's a big man, a man of respect. But I don't take crap from anyone else, outsiders. This isn't Washington, or New York, even. This is Naples, Italy, Naples that had the shit shelled and bombed out of it, Naples where everybody hustles to stay god-damned alive!' The anger went out of his voice, and he spoke softly again. 'Me, I hustle too. Different level, maybe. I do a friend a favour, fine, maybe one day he does me one. You, you're not my friend, and you want a favour you can't pay back. So I settle for cash. *Capisce?*'

'*Capito,*' Rafferty said. 'Sorry.'

Esposito grinned like a shark. 'That's the boy, Jim,' he said.

'I don't have that kind of money with me,' Rafferty told him.

'Shush, don't worry about it, I trust you, I trust you,' Esposito said.

'You give it to the driver when he takes you back to your hotel, right? No sweat. I know you wouldn't try to renege.'

He put the folder in Rafferty's hands.

'It's all in there,' he said. 'Everything you need. Okay?'

61

'Okay,' Rafferty said. 'One more thing.' Esposito raised his eyebrows.

'You never saw me,' Rafferty told him. 'You never heard of James Lawrence. He was never in Naples. Never even in Italy. Got it?'

'Sure, sure,' Esposito said. His eyes were hooded behind the tinted lenses. Rafferty couldn't see any expression there at all. He shrugged mentally. It was a calculated risk, one he was going to have to take. With his neck stuck this far out, another inch didn't really make that much difference anyway.

5

Zürich, Switzerland
12 June 1945

The Hotel Bristol on the Stampfenbach-strasse is a small, unobtrusive bed-and-breakfast hotel — what they call an *hôtel garni* — frequented by commercial travellers and middle-class businessmen. It is set back away from the street, which slopes sharply down towards the lake, its main entrance approached up a wide flight of stone steps. Its rooms are simple, clean and functional.

Two men sat in room 47, on the fourth floor. The curtains were drawn although it was not dark outside. Once in a while they could hear the clattering roar of a tram going up the hill.

'You know why I am here,' Rafferty said.

'Yes,' was the reply. 'I had word . . . from Naples.'

'May we get straight to business, Mr Shelley?'

'By all means.'

The man called Shelley looked very ordinary. Tall, slim, about thirty-five, Rafferty judged. His clothes were decent, but not first class. His hair was sandy brown, his eyes green, skin lightly tanned, smooth shaven. He smoked French cigarettes which he lit with a battered GI Zippo lighter. His hands were long fingered, slim and tapered, and Rafferty put his weight around 150 pounds, give or take a little.

'Good,' Rafferty said, and lifted his briefcase off the floor by the table, opening it and taking a photograph out. He put the photo — a 10 × 8 glossy — on the table. Shelley looked at it.

'An American general,' he said. It was not a question, and there was not a trace of surprise in his voice.

'Brigadier-General George Campion,' Rafferty said. 'Presently the Military Governor of Bavaria.'

'I see,' Shelley said, waiting.

To his own surprise, Rafferty found he

was having difficulty in framing the way he was going to say what he had to say. Shelley gave him no help at all. He waited, lighting another cigarette. Rafferty wrinkled his nostrils: the damned things smelled foul. He couldn't understand why anyone would choose to smoke them.

'It is necessary,' Rafferty finally came up with, 'to complete the assignment before Christmas.'

Shelley nodded, saying nothing.

'Can you do it?' Rafferty asked.

'Before I answer your question,' Shelley said, 'let me ask you one. What exactly is it that you want done?'

Rafferty let his breath out slowly. You bastard, he thought, you're not going to get me to put it into words of one syllable. For all I know this place could have more microphones in it than the NBC studios. He leaned forward, elbows on the table, and fixed Shelley's eyes with his own. He could see nothing in the eyes that returned his stare with complete equanimity. No apprehension, no amusement, no wariness, no unease, no warmth

— nothing. They were just eyes. For seeing with.

'It is essential,' Rafferty said slowly, 'that you arrange things so that there will be no hint of your involvement. It must look like an accident. What kind of an accident I leave to you. But under no circumstances whatsoever can it look like anything else. Is that clear, Mr Shelley?'

'Perfectly,' Shelley said. 'Anything else?'

'Yes,' Rafferty bored in, 'there is. If there is any way of assuring it, you must try to effect your assignment outside the immediate area in which the subject has his command.'

'I see,' Shelley said. 'Does he travel a great deal?'

'Not a great deal,' Rafferty replied. 'But enough.'

He opened his briefcase and brought out a plain buff folder which he slid across the table.

'This should provide you with what you need,' he said.

Shelley opened the folder and ran his eyes over the first page. He turned it back and scanned the next and then the next.

'Admirable,' he said.

'Biographical data, background information, personal habits, names of staff, everything I could think of.'

'Very thorough,' Shelley said. 'I take it there isn't another copy?'

Rafferty shook his head. 'Typed it myself,' he replied. 'No carbon.'

Shelley leaned back in his chair, putting his hands behind his head and flexing the muscles of his shoulders.

'It is an unusual assignment,' he said, finally. 'But I think it can be done. Yes, I think so.'

'How will you . . . ?'

Shelley held up a hand and smiled.

'At this stage, I have no ideas, but even if I had, I should not discuss them with you at all,' he said. 'You have someone you want killed and you have come to me because you have been assured of my professional expertise. Now either you accept the recommendations you were given or you do not. If you do not, then you have only to get up and walk out.'

'Yes,' Rafferty said. 'But you will understand my need for an assurance that the assignment will be carried out before the deadline.'

'You have my assurance of that,' Shelley said, with such dignity and sincerity that for a moment, Rafferty was prompted to apologise. Then he remembered that he was dealing with a hired assassin and his intention evaporated instantly.

'What about the fee?' he said, roughly.

'Fifty thousand dollars in advance,' Shelley said. 'And another twenty five thousand on completion of the assignment,' He smiled faintly.

'You see there is an element of trust required on my part, too.'

'Seventy five thousand dollars,' Rafferty said, slowly. 'That's high.'

'I think you were advised that my services did not come cheap, Mr Lawrence,' Shelley said. 'You will notice that I do not ask you who you are, or why you want this general killed. Whatever your reasons, political or monetary, I assume that you will profit in some way by his death. My silence as to your intentions and motives also costs money.'

'You're threatening me?' Rafferty said.

'No, no, Mr Lawrence,' Shelley said. 'Merely reminding you that we are discussing a partnership. When my part of it is finished, you will never hear from me or of me again. You are guaranteed of that fact by the people through whom you found me. And that is why you must pay the price I ask. After all,' he finished disarmingly, 'I can hardly sue you for breach of contract if you disown me, as you will most certainly do should I be caught while trying to do what you want me to do.'

'God forbid,' Rafferty said, fervently.

'Mr Lawrence, I wouldn't have lasted ten minutes in this business had I ever been slipshod. For instance,' he said, lighting yet another Gitane, 'I know that you will check up on me, and I know what you will find out.'

Rafferty began to speak, but again Shelley held up the peremptory hand.

'It's perfectly all right, Mr Lawrence,' he said.

'Let me simply assure you that the moment this assignment is over, the identity which you will so painstakingly uncover will be discarded by me. It is part of my life — indeed, you could say my life literally depends upon it — to ensure that there are no means by which I can be traced in the normal police manner. I tell you this not out of vanity, but simply to encourage you to leave well enough alone. People remember being asked questions about other people. So accept me for what you think I am, and leave it at that. Do I make myself clear?'

'Perfectly,' Rafferty said, a trace of annoyance in his voice.

'Good,' Shelley said. 'Now: how many people besides yourself are party to knowledge about me and this assignment?'

'Myself and one other. Perhaps two. No one else.'

'You say perhaps two. You are not sure?'

'I would say two others besides myself.'

'And no one else? No members of your staff, no Embassy employees, no State Department people?'

Rafferty shook his head. 'No one.'

'Good,' Shelley said. 'Then we can proceed. This is what you will do. Some time in the next twenty-four hours — it

70

doesn't matter when — you will place a briefcase containing fifty thousand dollars in used notes, none of which is to be of a higher denomination than fifty dollars, in locker 14B in the left-luggage lockers on the north side of the Hauptbahnhof here in Zürich. Here,' he pushed an envelope across the table, 'is the key to that locker. You will not have the locker watched, nor will you attempt to have me followed. I will know it if you do, and warn you that such an attempt will seriously jeopardise our relationship. I hope I make myself understood?'

'You do,' Rafferty said. 'Don't worry, I'll do as you say.'

'Good,' Shelley said, getting to his feet. 'As soon as you have put the money into the locker, I will begin work. There is only one other thing. How can I contact you if I need to?'

'You'll find a telephone number in the dossier I gave you on Campion,' Rafferty said. 'It's a Frankfurt number. You will identify yourself as Shelley. The person who answers your call will reply 'Keats'. If he does not, you ring off immediately.'

'Satisfactory,' Shelley said, 'I doubt I shall need to use it, but it is as well to have it.'

Rafferty got up, and picked up his briefcase. Shelley opened the door for him and he went out into the corridor, walked down the stairs and came out into the busy street. People were coming out of offices, and there were waiting crowds on the islands by the tram stop. He crossed the street and walked down the hill a way, turning into a small cafe that nestled in the right angle of two buildings. Taking a seat by the window, he ordered coffee. At the next table there was a thickset man in a fur collared overcoat, wearing one of the wide-brimmed hats the Swiss seem to favour. He was reading the *Neue Zürcher Zeitung*. Without looking at him, Rafferty spoke softly, hardly moving his lips.

'Room 47, name of Peter Shelley. Five nine or ten, hundred and fifty, sixty, pounds; sandy-brown hair, green eyes, dark-blue suit, white shirt, black shoes. Smokes Gitanes.'

The man reading the newspaper did

not betray by the flicker of an eyelid that Rafferty had spoken, but after a few moments called for his check, paid the waitress and went out into the street. He walked up the hill to where a car was parked outside a watchmaker's shop opposite the Bristol Hotel. As he passed it, he slapped his leg with the folded newspaper, then crossed the street behind the car, looking carefully left and then right as he did so. Behind him, two men got out of the Volkswagen and locked it, crossing the street and keeping pace with the first man, perhaps sixty feet behind him. Within ten minutes of Rafferty's leaving the Bristol, it was under surveillance front and back. There was no exit from which Shelley could leave without being seen by one of the three OSS men from Berne. They waited there all through the night and next morning reported that no sign of Shelley had been seen. Rafferty told them to have a maid check discreetly, and she came back with the information that the Herr Shelley had checked out of the hotel immediately after he had been visited by an American gentleman.

6

Frankfurt
15 June 1945

'It's on, then?'

Walt Gilchriese leaned back in the
swivel chair behind his desk, his habitual
wet-ended cigar stuck in the side of his
mouth. He was a beefy, balding, flabby
man with wide shoulders and a broken
nose as mementoes of his days as an
All-American. As Executive Officer in the
Communications Division of SHAEF his
power was almost — but not quite — as
great as that of Colonel Donald Rogers,
who sat now with one hip hoisted on the
corner of Gilchriese's desk. Where Rogers
was the lean, mean-looking member of
the duo who spoke no more than he had
to, Gilchriese was extrovert, boisterous,
sometimes even crude, but fast on his feet
the way that big men sometimes surprisingly are. Between them they kept the

Supreme Commander of the Allied Expeditionary Forces, General Dwight D. Eisenhower, inside a fairly narrow spectrum of options. They screened him from all the do-gooders and freeloaders, from all the hype-merchants and wheeler-dealers who needed Ike's nod to get their tatty deals on the road. They refined and edited the masses of information and activity reports which came into SHAEF daily into neat and succinct reports, what they called 'option papers', which carefully and usually fairly presented the various choices open to 'the Old Man' — as they called him — and the feasible results which would ensue if any of those options were taken up. It was assumed by all who came into contact with them, and with good reason, that they spoke for the Supreme Commander. Certainly no one yet had had the temerity to challenge that assumption.

'On and running,' Rogers said. There was just the faintest hint of satisfied cleverness in his voice.

'And Rafferty?'

'Swallowed it like syrup of figs,' Rogers

said. 'He's paid this Shelley the money — and even better, let Shelley slip the lead in Zürich — done it all by the book, just like the good little soldier he is.'

'And now?'

'You know what 'and now',' Rogers said. 'We've discussed that.'

'There's no viable alternative?'

Rogers shook his head. 'No. He's the only link with us. With that link gone, there's no way this thing could ever be traced back to this office.'

'Reassure me,' Gilchriese grunted, shifting his bulk in the chair. It was warm in the big office on the fourteenth floor of the I.G. Farben building in Frankfurt which was the headquarters of SHAEF. The sun, magnified by the big glass windows, beat strongly into the room.

'For Christ's sake, Walt,' Rogers said testily.

'Reassure me,' insisted Gilchriese.

'Alright, alright,' Rogers agreed. 'The Oshawa meeting: Rafferty set it up. He was on leave. No record of my arrival there — in fact, my leave was taken in

Naples, and I can prove that's where I was.'

'Okay, so far,' Gilchriese grunted. 'Go on.'

'Rafferty made the meet with Luciano under an alias. No contact with us. Went to Italy and Zürich on his own business. Again, no contact here. Set the Shelley thing up alone. Nothing to do with us. Our only contact has been the phone call advising it was on. Untraceable, insofar as it connects us with it. We're clear.'

'Except for Rafferty himself,' Gilchriese said.

'Right,' Rogers agreed. 'Which is why we've got to play it like we agreed, all the way down the line.'

'Okay,' Gilchriese said. Then, 'I sure as hell hope you're right about this, Don.'

Rogers grinned. It was an untypical thing for him to do.

'You better believe it, baby,' he said. He unhitched his hip off the desk and went to the door, looking back as he opened it.

'I'll set it all up,' he said. 'Okay?'

Gilchriese sighed, and stubbed out the soggy cigar butt in the overflowing ashtray on his desk.

'Okay,' he said. 'Get it moving.'

The door closed behind Rogers and he reached automatically for the cigar humidor in front of him. Selecting one of the cigars he looked at it and then put it down. I'm smoking too many of these damned things, he thought. He thought of Mike Rafferty, whom he knew briefly, and wondered if the guy had any family. No, he thought. No, he hasn't, he's single, remembering the file Rogers had shown him on Rafferty when they had first set up what they referred to between themselves as the Oshawa Project. Rogers had gone to a lot of trouble to find just the right man for setting up the hit.

There was a knock on the door and a sergeant from the Communications Division poked his head around it as it opened.

'Meeting of all staff officers in the conference room at 1500 hours, sir,' he said.

'Okay, Sergeant,' Gilchriese said, lurching to his feet and pulling some papers together into a bundle with his huge paw. By the time he got to the door there was another cigar smouldering between his clamped lips.

7

Zürich
18 June 1945

The tram grated around the corner into the Paradeplatz and came to a stop, the doors jerking open with a sharp hiss, people hurrying down the steps and under the shelter of the concrete awning over the island. It was a drizzling day, and everyone was intent on keeping dry and getting where they were going, heads down against the cool rain. The flags hung listless, soaked, from their flagpoles along the Bahnhofstrasse. No one took any notice of the tall young man with the black attaché case who crossed the tramlines quickly and went into the entrance of the Schweizer Kreditverein at 14 Paradeplatz. The man stopped at the information desk in the hall of the bank, giving the young woman there his visiting card. She referred him to another clerk, who opened a door at the side of the long row of counters and led the way to the elevators, smiling friendlily as he indicated which direction to walk when they came to the third floor. The clerk led the sandy-haired visitor along a wide corridor and into one of the many rooms flanking it, closing the door behind him with a smile and a nod.

It was a small office with a desk and several functional modern chairs, one armchair, two Oriental rugs, a Mondrian print framed on the wall. On a small table beside the door were copies of *Neue Zürcher Zeitung*, the *Financial Times*, the *Wall Street Journal* and *Time Magazine*. The room was functional but antiseptic, like most Swiss business premises.

After a few minutes the door opened and a dark young man of about thirty came in. He was neatly dressed in a dark suit, white shirt, plain tie, and impeccably shined black shoes. His hair was straight and cut very short.

'*Gruezi*,' he said.

'My name is Shelley,' the visitor said.

'Peter Shelley. I'm American.'

'Oh, American,' the young man said. 'They told me English, and I was surprised. I am Würmli. A Swiss name.' He smiled, as though trying to put Shelley at his ease. His English was very good, although slightly accented in the Germanic manner.

'You wish to ask about numbered accounts,' he offered.

'That's right,' Shelley said.

'You are an American citizen, Mr Shelley?'

'Yes.'

'Then, it's good,' Würmli said, as though he were personally pleased. 'I will explain you our procedure.' He took a seat behind the desk and got some papers out of the drawer on the right-hand side, arranging them neatly in front of him. Then he took out a fountain pen and unscrewed the top, placing that to his right. He folded his hands, leaned forward on the desk and looked at Shelley.

'My bank will open a numbered account for you providing you make an initial deposit of not less than twenty-five thousand dollars American,' he began. 'It is the rule of my bank that we shall invest not less than one quarter of this sum in securities: Swiss, American, or other. This sum you are not allowed to draw until closing your account. This is also the Swiss law,' he said, smiling to explain that it wasn't something he had just thought up personally.

'If you wish to open such an account, you must present to us your passport at the time. We will like to know where the money will come from: this is particularly important in the present times, you understand. There are many regulations governing the movement of money into Switzerland — and out, too.'

Shelley nodded. 'I understand,' he said.

'You will be asked to declare whether you intend to pay tax in your own country on the money in your account, Mr Shelley,' Würmli continued. 'If you answer no, the bank will not open an account for you. If you answer yes, it will. The bank does not ask for evidence, however, that you have paid these taxes.

You understand this?'

'Perfectly,' Shelley said, thinking 'hypocritical bastards.'

'Under Swiss law, the bank is then bound by absolute secrecy as to your identity and the amount you hold in your account. If requested, the bank will hold all mail addressed to you in our care, and will not send mail to you unless you demand us to do so.'

'Is there any restriction upon the currency in which the account is kept?'

'None at all,' Würmli replied. 'Under certain circumstances, which it will be possible to explain to you later, the bank will pay a small interest on deposits also. However, if you choose to maintain your account in Swiss francs, there is a two per cent negative interest — this is also required by Swiss law.' He waved his hand to indicate again that the law was none of his doing.

'Who handles the account once it is opened?'

'There are only perhaps two or three persons in the bank who will know of your account with us, Mr Shelley,' the

Swiss said. 'Like a bank inside a bank. Normally one person will handle all transactions to do with your account. If you so wish, we can arrange for a code name to identify anything concerning it, and you may change the code name at any time if you wish additional security.'

'In what circumstances would the identity of a depositor be revealed?' Shelley asked, enjoying the look of pained horror which touched the clerk's face at the mere thought.

'Oh, but this is almost impossible to happen,' Würmli said.

'Just suppose,' Shelley insisted. 'For argument's sake.'

'If it was to be revealed that the money deposited had been stolen, or obtained by illegal means, *zum Bei* . . . I beg your pardon, for example — or if it can be legally shown that the money has been embezzled, then the bank is required by law to reveal the identity of the depositor.'

'Can further deposits be made by a third party, if necessary?'

'Not personally, Mr Shelly. Bank transfers, of course, are another thing.

But for personal deposits, the bank prefers that the depositor appears in person, unless in most unusual circumstances. Should such circumstances arise, as perhaps they may, then of course we shall arrange special instructions for identification, a special code, perhaps. Do you expect such a thing to be happening?'

'No,' Shelley said. 'I just wanted to know. Oh, one other thing: how soon after an account is opened can drafts be written against it?'

'Why, right away, sir,' said Würmli, almost offended by the question.

'Good,' Shelley said. 'Then we can get started?'

'Sir?'

Shelley reached down beside him and put the briefcase on the desk in front of the bank employee. He turned it around and opened it. It was full of money.

'Fifty thousand dollars,' he said.

To Würmli's credit, he didn't even blink.

'I will count it,' he said.

8

Munich
22 June 1945

You had to hand it to Rogers, Rafferty thought as he tooled the jeep through the shattered streets, when he pulled strings they stayed pulled. Time and again since he had left the States he had been surprised — no, he corrected himself, astonished — at the way in which everything had been laid on. Like clockwork, he thought. Travel permits not at all the easiest pieces of paper to come by in the devastated mess that was Europe, had been waiting for him on the dot. Transportation had been laid on without fuss, and never a question as to his purpose or his utilisation of it. He rather gathered, from one or two remarks he had overheard, that certain key people in each of the places he had found it necessary to visit had been given instructions and told to implement them, no questions asked. And they had been perfectly implemented with, in most cases, no more than a curious, covert glance. How they had achieved such perfect communications internally when everything else worked by the old army rule of Murphy's Law, in itself an extension of the philosophy best described in the words, 'you can't win', he neither knew nor cared to ask.

Frankly, he was glad the whole thing was over. He felt released from the strain of the past few weeks, the checking and cross-checking, the long hours of travelling, the waiting in military airfields for planes constantly feeling that someone, somewhere, was watching him (and he wouldn't have been surprised to find that Rogers had indeed got someone checking his movements), happily over. Now he drove through the devastated city, watching for MPs who would direct him away from streets where demolition of dangerous buildings was still proceeding, seeing the gangs of German men and women laboriously clearing bombed sites, picking up the broken bricks and masonry by hand, lugging them to handcarts, and in some cases even baby prams. He had heard somewhere that over seven thousand people had perished in the bombing of Munich. It was a desolate, desolated city, and he would be glad to get on the plane tonight that would take him to Paris. The thought of being back in the States by Wednesday was something to hang on to in this starving, shattered, beaten citadel of the destroyed Reich.

He turned the jeep into the Galeriestrasse, where he was using the apartment of a German who was conveniently away from Munich at this moment. From the few personal things Rafferty had found in the apartment, he had concluded that the man, whose name was Desch, was in the printing or newspaper business. What his debt to or connection with SHAEF was, Rafferty could not surmise, nor did he want to know.

He wondered what Shelley would do, and how he would finally kill Campion. Rafferty had no real feeling about the man who was to be Shelley's target. He did not know him, had never seen him. You'd have to have been deaf, dumb and blind not to have heard of him, of course, and certainly on the few occasions when he'd seen the man on newsreels he had found it difficult to reconcile the glowing eulogies to Campion's astonishing victories in battle and the thin-voiced, overdressed old man whose picture had been on the screen. Grey-haired, erect, Campion had been addressing a crowd in Los Angeles, somewhere. He looked coarse, gruff, professionally paternal, and the things he had said to the crowd had been banal, atrocious. He wondered what he would have thought watching that newsreel if he had known then what he now knew.

Rafferty stopped the jeep outside the house and set the emergency brake, checking to make sure there was nothing that could be lifted, taken, or torn loose in the vehicle. He didn't expect to be in the house long. By seven he had to be out at the airport, and then, oh that lovely plane to Paris. He opened the apartment door, which was on the ground floor, and went into the big room which doubled as living and bedroom. Beyond it was a kitchen and a small toilet. Not much, he thought, but in Munich right now, the purest of luxury. He'd have been happier staying at the Officers' Club, but there'd been no question of that. One of the earliest things Rogers had said was that he must avoid fraternisation with anyone. He thought guiltily for a moment of his evening drinks with the young sailor in Naples, then shrugged. Hinton probably wouldn't even remember his name, and even if he did, it was not the right name.

For all his years in intelligence work, Rafferty was a man of habit. He had set ways of doing things which he had no idea were set ways, but which others, who knew him, realised. Thus, as he had done on the other occasions he had come into the apartment, he went across to the windows and drew back the curtains. He had closed them when he went out earlier to exclude the sun so that the room would stay at least nominally cool; the window faced due south, looking out at the shell of a building that had once housed shops. He could still make out the fire-twisted word *Bäckerei* above one of the yawning empty spaces that had been the shop window. Above the empty shops, the shell of what had been the living quarters, roofless now and gutted, turned empty windows like eyeless sockets towards the silent street.

As he pulled back the curtains, the man lying on his belly in the rubble of the upstairs rooms of the bakery across the street caught Rafferty squarely in the cross hairs of the telescopic sight on the 7.92 mm Falschirmäger Gewehr 42, a wartime parachutist's rifle first produced in 1942 by Rheinmetall. It was hardly the ideal sniper's rifle, for it had always been a difficult gun to shoot accurately, but the man behind it had only about sixty feet to shoot over, and the telescopic sight brought the second button on Rafferty's tunic close enough for him to feel he could reach out and touch it. His first shot smashed the glass window to whickering, splintering fragments, killing the bullet, which whined off sideways. His next shot, a fraction of a second later, left the twenty-inch barrel at a speed of half a mile a second, tearing into Rafferty's heart, smashing him backwards across the room and over the top of a sofa standing facing the window, a hole as big as a dinner plate in his back where the bullet had exited, blood spraying up to spatter the grubby, off-white ceiling and the wallpaper with its faded sycamore-leaf pattern. He died knowing, without ever really forming the thought, why Rogers had insisted he return via Munich.

Across the street the man in the bombed house slapped the tripod flat beneath the barrel of the gun, unscrewed the clumsy silencer and detached the plastic butt of the rifle. Then he stowed the whole thing into a long cardboard box of the kind florists use, battered now but with the word *Kranzlerblumen* still visible in faded script on the lid. He fastened the box with two webbing straps and carefully made his way down the remnants of the stairway, climbing agilely over the gaping holes to the ground floor.

He came out slowly into the street at the far end through the broken shells of other houses, checking in each direction. Then he hurried into the Ludwigstrasse, mingling with the slow-moving crowd. He did not know who he had killed, or why. All he knew was that there were two thousand crisp new dollars in the envelope he had carefully hidden behind the bricks of what had once been the fireplace of his mother's house in Schwabing, and that with the money, and some luck, he might now be able to get Lisl to come with him, out of Berlin, back here to Bavaria.

9

Madrid
16 July 1945

On the day that the scientists at Los Alamos, New Mexico, test-exploded that first atomic bomb, 'brighter than a thousand suns', two men were sitting at a table along one of the long walls of the Jockey restaurant. It is a somewhat exclusive and fairly expensive place, long and narrow as you enter, with a wider room to your right. There are sporting prints of gaily-shirted riders on spindly-legged thoroughbreds here and there. One of the men was old. Spry still, but nearing the danger mark of seventy-five summers. His companion was much younger: thirty-five, perhaps, not more. The old man's name was José Miguel Sedillo, and he was recalling how, in his youth, the great ballroom of the Grand Hotel in Vienna had been a centre of beauty and culture which had not bowed even to Paris for lovely women and high fashion.

'Ah, the Hussars and the Cavalry officers,' he sighed. 'They were so splendid. No good at all for war, you comprehend, but in the ballrooms, quite magnificent. I used to stay then in a hotel on the Stefansplatz. It was so pretty, so pretty. But then came the War, and it was all gone. I went back only once, in 1919, I think — my God, all those years ago! There were only two taxis in all of Vienna — and one of those was a *fiacre*, with a terrible old horse to pull it. I was glad to have Spanish money in those days, my friend. The hard times had come, and the Reichsmark went spinning, spinning, mad, quite insane. I remember staying at the best hotel in Nürnberg. Ach, do you know what I paid for a fine meal then? Three and a half pesetas! I gave them five and instantly became the most popular guest in the place. Five pesetas!'

He drank a little of the *Vina Ardanza*, and his companion poured some more into both glasses, sipping some himself. It was like Chianti, perhaps smoother.

'But all of this must be boring for you, my friend, the recollections of an old man.'

'No, not at all, Don José,' his companion said. 'It delights me. Tell me, were you in Paris after the First War?'

'Yes, once or twice,' the old man said. 'I never liked the place much — forgive me, I know it is your home — but ah, Paris was so pretty then. They had those huge Percherons to pull the buses, great beautiful animals. Alas, Paris has changed twice in this century, my friend. After the First War she went from good to bad. After this, when the Americans bring us their Coca-Cola civilisation, she will go from bad to impossible. As no doubt will Spain and the rest of Europe. I think that I have been fortunate to have lived when I did, and I am doubly fortunate that I will not have to live much longer. I leave the harder times ahead to younger men like yourself.'

'I envy you,' the younger man said, and there was no doubt of the sincerity in his voice. He signalled the waiter and ordered coffee and brandy, his eyes briefly touching the faces of the people at the tables near them. The restaurant had the comfortable air of a place never touched by the hot breath of real war, but he remembered Madrid in 1939. It had been very different then, the first time he had met the old man.

'The food was good, was it not?' Sedillo asked.

'Extremely.'

They had eaten green noodles grainé, canard à l'orange, wild raspberries. Now with the coffee they brought petit fours.

Sedillo picked up his brandy and sniffed it delicately.

'Spanish, I fear,' he said. 'It is impossible to get good French brandy.

'Those Nazi crooks stole it all. They say the chef here used to cook for Goering, you know. I don't know if it's true. It probably is. Most of those stories are.'

The young man nodded. They made an unlikely pair, the old gentleman in his dark-blue lightweight suit, his olive skin furrowed with the years of his life, and the calm, dark-haired younger man with the pale-blue eyes and sturdy, capable-looking body. Anyone watching them might have thought them perhaps distant relatives, one of the younger ones from far away visiting his great-uncle, or perhaps an honoured god-father.

In fact the purpose of their meeting was to discuss the making of a gun. Don José was one of the finest craftsmen in Spain. A dealer all his life in antique firearms, specialising in Brescian pistols, he had once shown his companion a pair of beautifully ornamented pistols by Lazarino Cominazzo with snaphaunce locks, nestling in their original case, which were the pride of his extensive collection and truly priceless. Although he was officially retired, Don José still loved to work on something 'special'. An intricately chased set of pistols, perhaps, intended to be given by some ambassador to another, copied from the designs of someone like Nicholas Noel Boutet, *Directeur Artiste à Versailles* and gunsmith to Louis XVI and Napoleon, whose stature had been so great that he had been spared in the blood bath of the Revolution. Sedillo could talk fascinatingly for hours about the great gunsmiths: the Manton brothers of London; Durs Egg, the Swiss master; Wogdon, Mortimer, Rigby of Dublin; Forsyth, the Scottish minister who had invented the fulminating lock; Henry Deringer and the Hawkens in America — he was a never-ending, encyclopaedic source of stories and information about them.

The old man put down his empty brandy glass and shook his head at the raised-eyebrow offer of another.

'No, my young friend,' he said. 'We must talk now of your problem.'

'I would be honoured,' the younger man said.

'It is an intriguing problem you set me,' Sedillo said. 'Such a weapon has never been made, I think.'

'Can it be made?'

'Everything can be made, my dear André,' Sedillo said. 'With time, and patience, everything.'

'It must be light,' André said. 'Small, if possible. Easy to carry.'

'Tush, these are details,' Sedillo said. 'Easily encompassed. It is the matter of the ammunition for which you ask. This is something I have not encountered before.'

He pursed his lips, wise old eyes searching the face of the younger man beside him.

'I must ask you a delicate question, my young friend,' he said. 'As I have done before. I must have some idea of what your target will be, what range you must shoot over.'

'A man,' was the reply. 'At about fifty feet.'

Sedillo nodded, his face a little sadder than before.

'Why not a conventional bullet?'

'I cannot explain that.'

The old man nodded, as much as to say he had not expected an explanation.

'How many shots?'

'Not more than two. There will be no time for more. If they are not enough, twenty would not do it.'

'Standing, or at rest?'

'At rest, I think.'

'I see. And the ammunition, yes, the ammunition. I have to think most carefully upon this. It is of a great difference. And it is sometimes difficult these days to get synthetic materials.'

'I appreciate that. And you know if I can assist you, you have but to ask.

'Yet I must know very soon whether it can be done.'

'You know now it can be done, my dear André,' the old man smiled. 'You knew that before you came to me, Sedillo, you said to yourself, can make it. And he can,' he said, smiling slightly, patting the younger man's forearm with a liver-spotted hand.

'We will meet again one week from now, if that will be agreeable.'

'I shall be honoured,' the man called André said.

'Yes, yes,' the old man replied, already far away in his thoughts, working on the problem his companion had set him, his old eyes shining with anticipation. 'Come, finish your drink and let us go.'

André picked up his drink and raised his glass to Don José Miguel.

'*Salud, pesetas y amor,*' he said. 'Health, money and love.'

'*Y el tiempo,*' the old man replied. 'And the time to enjoy them.'

10

Berlin
21 July 1945

Liselotte Klatt lay naked on the grubby bed in her cellar room. Beside her, Werner snored gently in the rosy nirvana of after-sex. Pig, she thought. She had taken no pleasure, no pleasure at all, in his urgent lovemaking, his whispered endearments; but she had pretended passion during the act, making small sounds of ecstasy, scratching his naked skin, making herself shudder too as he reached his climax, his body arching and a long groaning sound of utter gratification coming from his gasping mouth. Ugly pig, she thought. The American boys were so much nicer. Younger, too, she added mentally, remembering the flabby feel of Werner's spreading midriff under her hands. She reached for the pack of Chesterfields on the wooden box that served her for a bedside table. At least he had brought cigarettes. As she lit the cigarette, inhaling greedily, she thought once more of what he had told her when he came that night. The decrepit room she called home was a cellar beneath a pile of rubble which had once been an apartment house on the Tirolerstrasse, a hundred yards or so from Pankow U-Bahn station. She shared it with another girl — woman, really — who was on the game. Werner had given Marti fifty dollars to stay out all night. Fifty dollars! Her eyes had widened at first, then sharpened shrewdly as he had fumbled the money into Marti's hands. There had to be more where that came from, and so she played along, waiting. She worked during the day as a waitress in a cafe in the American zone, returning each night to the cellar, which was just inside the Russian sector. It didn't bother Lisl much: the Russian guards knew her face. They liked blondes and she rarely had much trouble with them, apart from one or two who always put their hands where they had no business putting them, but she played along, up to a point, letting her simple blonde prettiness work for her. She had a child's mind; if she could get what she wanted with her face and her body, Lisl was going to get it. There were precious few other ways for a girl to keep body and soul together in Berlin these days.

Although she would have slapped the face of anyone who called her a whore (she was the kind of girl who believed that ladies slapped the faces of men who displeased them, a belief resulting from an almost endless diet of very bad films) Lisl had few scruples about selling her body for the favours that American soldiers could give her. Gum, candy, liquor, cigarettes, clothes — especially silk stockings, everyone seemed to want silk stocking or nylons — all these were as good as gold on the scavenger-filled streets of the ruined capital. Lisl had no intention of starving to death, waiting for providence to give her a handout. The war had not been all that bad, except the last year or so. Berlin had been quite a place in the old days. But when the tide turned, and things got harder, as food grew scarce and even the SS officers couldn't get her ration coupons any more, Lisl had on more than one occasion let some well-fed businessman pick her up in the cafe, and gone back with him to his hotel room. She had stayed in hiding for almost a month when the Russians captured the city. There were stories of women being raped everywhere. And then it was all over. The city was divided, like a cake. There had been a brief liaison with a Russian soldier, some kind of officer. He had got her this place, apologising to her that it was the best he could do. Shortly after he had left Berlin for duty in Prague or somewhere god-forsaken like that, she had met Werner Linz.

He had winked at her from his table in the cafe on the Kudamm as she walked by on the way home from work. She always walked along the Kudamm because anyone who could afford to pay what they charged in the cafes for *ersatz* coffee and even worse *Strudel* might be, well, a possibility. She would never have permitted herself to think of them in the robust terms of some of the women she knew: Marti called them 'Fritzes' — to her they were all called Fritz.

She had bridled, simpered, but gone across to his table, the other girl she'd been walking with continuing on her way alone. She put what she thought was a cheeky smile on her face, and it had touched Werner's heart because she looked so pathetic and so lost.

'Sit, sit,' he had said. 'Take something.'

His German was accented. Bavarian, she had decided. She wasn't like a lot of the Northerners, she quite liked the softer, more musical cadences of the Bavarian dialect.

She didn't really listen to the story he had told her then. She always forgot what they said, anyway. It was a kind of revenge for what they did to her body. But it had been something about war graves, something like that. He came to Berlin regularly, he said. He had taken her out to places where Germans were able to go, once or twice to poor substitutes for restaurants where they were allowed in when he showed them some papers he carried. Later, he'd suggested a more permanent arrangement, and had begun to visit her regularly at the cellar room, sometimes twice a month, a day or two at a time. Finally he told her he loved her and wanted to marry her, and it had been all she could do not to laugh. Now, she was glad she hadn't. Things were very bad in Berlin. There were strict rules about fraternisation. Some of the soldiers ignored them, of course, they wanted their *Schätzi*, laws or no laws. But the Military Police were getting very tough with anyone who defied the military laws, and when they did burst in you were into prison faster than you could say Pankow. The only thing that Lisl was interested in was whether Werner had as much money as he'd hinted. Enough, he'd said, to get them a new life somewhere in a part of the world where you didn't have to live like a rat in a sewer. He said there was a sergeant at Marienborn he could bribe. All they had to do was get through the checkpoint here, and that wouldn't be too difficult if she would flirt with the guards as they were checked through.

As she had done many times before, Lisl wondered what Werner did for a living. That stuff he had fed her about war graves was rubbish, *unsinnig*. She remembered when he had talked in his sleep that time, tossing sweatily on the bed, muttering about getting people, the gun, the gun, he'd kept on repeating the word, the muttering dying away, one repeated word hanging in the silence as he went back to sleep, *Blut, Blut Blut* — blood. She thought he was some kind of gangster — those films again — and in fact that was the nearest she ever came to knowing what Werner Linz really was: a paid cut-throat. Well, she thought now, whatever he is, he has money. You could live very nicely in Berlin if you had plenty of money.

Lisl eased herself quietly off the bed, padding naked across the dirty floor to the chair upon which he had thrown his clothes in an impatient tangle. There was nothing but loose change in the pants, some keys, a crumpled dollar bill. She went towards the door, where his leather jacket hung on a nail. In the right-hand pocket she found a wadded bundle of papers held together with an elastic band. There was a Swiss passport in the name of Werner Linz, born Basle, 3 March 1909, and two German identity cards, one in her name and the other in the name of Heinrich Alton. But it was Werner's photograph affixed to it. She stared at the dog-eared pieces of card. Where had he got them? Where had he got the photograph of her — God, she looked awful! She knew — you could not live in Berlin and not know — that it was possible to buy forged identity cards. She also knew, instinctively, that they cost a great deal of money. She remembered now about the photographs. There had been an old man near the Brandenburgertor, and he had an old camera that stood on three wooden legs. There was a can with some liquid in it underneath the antique old camera, and they had waited while he developed the pictures on some kind of tin, sticking them in clumsily-made cardboard frames and charging the earth for them. The one of her had been awful, and Werner had stuck them in his pocket, grinning. He must have had a print made from that, she thought. My God, he must have done some paying out! In the inside pocket of the jacket on the right-hand side she found a wallet jammed full of banknotes: Swiss francs, and dollars, hundreds and hundreds of dollars. She caught her breath. It was the largest amount of money she had ever seen in her life.

Lisl froze as Werner shifted in his sleep and groaned, her arm coming up in a defensive reflex gesture. As it did, she hit something hard in the jacket and, frowning, she looked in the other inside pocket. Her hand touched metal, the shape impossible to mistake for anything else. She pulled out the gun. It was short-barrelled, oily, ugly. She knew nothing about guns except that carrying them in the Russian sector was an offence punishable by death. She bit her lip, panicking slightly, her mind racing. Without really thinking it through at all, she came to her decision.

As quietly as she could, she started to

get dressed, taking the wallet she had laid to one side and pushing it deep into the side pocket of the smart little two-piece suit he had bought her once, and which he liked her to wear. She tiptoed towards the bed, bending down, holding her breath, her hand groping for her shoes. Her face was inches away from his when his eyes opened. She screamed and he was awake in an instant.

'Lisl . . . *Gott*! What is it?'

'Nothing, darling, nothing,' she said. She tried to make her voice soothing, but it came out breathless, terrified. 'I was just going to . . . to buy . . . some food for us. Something to eat, darling . . . '

He just looked at her and read the whole thing on her stricken face. Lisl screeched in panic as he rolled off the bed, naked and menacing, rage knotting his heavy brows. He took hold of her hair in one great paw, pulling her head back and forcing a yawping scream from her throat. Then he pushed her away from him, with contemptuous force. She reeled across the room and the edge of the bed caught her behind her knees. She went over backwards on to the bed, legs up in the air. Werner was already patting the pockets of his jacket.

'Where is it?' he said. His voice was flat and cold and without any emphasis at all. He might have been asking the time. Lisl looked into his eyes and saw something there that terrified her. She sat up, trying to rearrange her clothes, her hand going out towards him.

'*Liebchen*,' she faltered. 'I was . . . I just wanted . . . '

'*Hure!*' he spat. 'The money!'

Lisl groped into her disarrayed clothes and pulled out the wallet. It snagged on the edge of her pocket and she tugged at it, making little whimpering sounds of panic, trying to pull it clear. Linz crossed the room, sudden anger darkening his face. He took hold of the wallet and his impatient pull ripped the jacket apart, the pocket tearing loose with an angry sound. Lisl looked at the jagged tear and suddenly her eyes filled with tears of rage. Her jacket! It was the only decent one she had! She mewed in senseless, childlike temper, bounding like a cat off the bed and at the naked man, her hands clawed, the long painted fingernails raking vivid red welts down his cheek. Bright blood trickled down the left side of his face and Lisl stepped back aghast, her mouth open with surprise at what she had done. In the same moment, Linz gave a roar of astonished rage and back-handed the girl away from him. He was a strong man, thickset and muscular, and the girl took the sweeping force of his clenched fist just below her fragile jawline. Linz heard, felt, the thin snap as the delicate machinery in her throat was smashed. She fell back against the bed, down on her knees on the grubby floor, her body drunken and asprawl. She tried to make some sound in her ruined throat, her eyes rolling up in her head horribly as she struggled desperately to suck air into her lungs through the paralysed muscles. She rolled over on her face, arms flailing, legs kicking in agony, her fingernails scrabbling on the bare floorboards, thin lines of blood marking the bizarre skittering movements of her hands. Linz stood, paralysed, watching her for long, awful seconds in which he could not move to help her, did not want to, ached to, then no longer could. Lisl's movements had changed now, slowly, slowly, no longer frantic and desperate but slower, like the movements of a swimmer tired from battling against a strong undertow. Linz ground his teeth together and stood and watched Lisl die, watched as she quivered and then stretched out slowly, the body deflating slightly, seeming as he watched to go flatter, closer to the ground.

He knelt quickly beside her and put a finger to the carotid artery below her ear. There was a faint pulse that ceased as he found it. He rolled her over. The doll-pretty face was distorted, the eyes wide, bulging, and the tongue protruding from her mouth like some obscene black sausage.

Think, he commanded his mind. *Think*!

He looked around the shabby room, a little of his habitual calm returning. Methodically he began to put on his clothes, his mind working furiously as he did so. He checked his pockets. The gun was still there. Then he went over the room very carefully, wiping any smooth surface that might have taken his fingerprints. He put the cigarettes and candy he had brought for Lisl into a paper sack and set it beside the door, ready to take with him. Finally, with a great deal of effort (*my God, was she stiffening already?*) he rolled Lisl's body beneath the bed. It would have to do. From the doorway nothing could be seen but the disarrayed bed. It would perhaps be two or three hours before Marti came back. If she came back at all: she might have been lucky and found a Fritz.

He picked up the paper bag and let himself out, climbing up the broken stone steps to the street and hurrying down the Tirolerstrasse. He turned left and hurried through the Kleingarten, skirting the flickering fires of the homeless who slept there, slowing when he reached the busier Bornholmerstrasse. Ahead he could see the dim light of the S-Bahn green in the darkness. Beyond it was the checkpoint. A few more minutes and he'd be through — they never bothered one much there.

There was a small line of people waiting by the black-and-white-striped hut. He joined it, shuffling along behind an old lady carrying a string bag with old clothes in it. The Russian guard, a Schmeisser slung across his shoulder, waved her through and Linz looked up, automatically moving to follow her. The Russian guard held up a hand.

'*Nyet!*' he said.

The Schmeisser was slipped off his shoulder and pointing at Linz. He frowned, puzzled.

'*Bitte?*'

'*Warten hier!*' the Russian said. He shouted something over his shoulder to the other guard, who nodded and went into the hut. Linz watched, helpless, a cold trickle of perspiration working its way down the centre of his chest beneath his clothes. One never knew with the Russians. The black-and-white-pole was down across the narrow space between the concrete blocks which had been set up, staggered left and right to prevent anyone making a run for the American sector, perhaps four hundred yards away.

Linz could see the hoarding with its four-language sign: 'You are now entering the American Zone.' He wished he was, but the distance might just as well have been four hundred miles. It was planned to render a dash across the neutral zone impossible. He shrugged; the man wasn't born who could outrun a short burst from a Schmeisser. As he moved, his arm touched the bulge beneath his jacket. *The gun*! My God, if they search me, he thought. He looked wildly left and right, trying to think of somewhere he could drop the gun without being seen. Nowhere: the area in front of the control post was as bare as a runway. And even as he formed the thought, the Russian guard came out and said something to the one watching Linz.

'*Kommen herein*!' he snapped, and Linz grimaced. Why couldn't any of them speak decent German? He went with the guard into the hut. There was another soldier standing behind the door, an old Moissin-Nagant 7.62 rifle at port across his chest. The room was bare except for a huge photograph of Stalin behind the desk where an officer wearing the insignia of a captain in the Red Army sat. He was quite young, his hair cut *en brosse* the way so many of them had it, high Slavic cheekbones and a mouth like a wound.

'*Papiere!*' he snapped, making an impatient gesture with his hand. The soldier behind Linz shoved him forward roughly. He just managed not to sprawl across the desk.

'*Papiere, schnell, schnell!*'

Linz fumbled in his pocket and handed him the German identity card which bore the name Heinrich Alton, metalworker, resident in Osnabruckstrasse, across the Spree from what was left of the old Schlossgarten.

'*Was machten Sie in diesem Sektor?*'

'*Ich besuchte eine Freundin,*' Linz said, putting that *you know* expression on his face. 'I was visiting a lady friend.'

The Russian did not reply. He looked at the identity card for a long time and then looked up at Linz.

'*Und Ihr Gesicht?*'

Linz frowned. My face? '*Bitte?*' he said.

'*Ja, ja, ja, Ihr Gesicht. Sie haben Blut*

auf Ihr Gesicht und Hemd. Was haben Sie gemacht?'

Linz' hand flew to his face, feeling the raw scratches. Damn her! He tried to keep the stupid smile going although he felt as if his jaw muscles might lock from the strain.

'*Ach*,' he said, deprecatingly, waving a hand to show it was nothing. '*Ein Unfall.*'

'An accident?' said the Russian coldly, raising his eyebrows just enough to show his disbelief.

'Yes, yes, only that,' Linz confessed eagerly. 'We were . . . you know, you're a man of the world. She does it to me sometimes. It sort of, gets me . . . worked up. You know.'

'Yes?' the Russian said. He made it sound as if Linz had just confessed to molesting five-year-old children.

'Yes, yes, just a little playfulness. She's a little vixen, that one.'

'She must be,' the Russian said, dryly. 'And her address?'

'Her address?'

'If you would be so kind,' said the Russian with heavy sarcasm.

'Oh, sir, you wouldn't . . . She has an old mother, very ill. She — '

'You are wasting my time.' There was an absolute lack of warmth in the man's voice and Linz flinched.

'Lodenbergstrasse. 23 Lodenbergstrasse.'

'Name?'

'Schneider. Renate Schneider.'

'So.' The officer got up from behind the desk and Linz saw that he was a short man. Somehow this seemed a good omen, although he couldn't think why.

'Wait in there,' the Russian said, waving towards a door on one side of the office. The guard who had brought Linz in opened the door and shoved him into the room. It was empty except for two benches by the wall. There was an army recruiting poster on the wall with graffitti in Russian pencilled on it. Nothing else.

'May I smoke?' he asked the officer, who was standing in the doorway watching him.

'By all means,' the man said. 'We will all smoke.' He took the pack of Chesterfields from Linz, looked at it and then into Linz' face. With a cold smile he took out one cigarette and tossed it to Linz, then flicked the pack across the room to the guard, who caught it deftly, grinning to show a mouthful of stained metal teeth. Then the door was slammed and Linz was alone in the night of his own fear. He could hear the officer dialling on the phone, but he spoke Russian and Linz knew only a few words of the language. He looked at his watch. 8.30. By nine he was longing for another cigarette, and more worried than he had ever been in his life. By ten he was terrified. When they kept you this long it was trouble, big trouble, because they were checking up on you. It would not take them long to discover there was no Renate Schneider at the address he had given them — if such an address existed in the rubbled ruins at all. He touched the gun in his pocket again, his mind skittering about like a rat in a maze. There was no window in the room, no cupboard, nowhere to hide the weapon. He prowled around the room, looking into the corners behind the benches. The floor was bare and musty and looked as if

122

it had not been swept for a long time. Taking the gun out of his pocket he poked with the barrel at the floorboards where they joined the wall. In one corner they were rotted. He pushed harder with the gun barrel and felt the wood yield, breaking up. Within a few frantic minutes he had made a hole big enough to slip the gun into. He sighed as he heard it thump on the ground beneath the floorboards. Now he took the money out of his pocket. He looked at it sadly. There was no way he could conceal it. When he was searched — and he felt certain he would be searched now — he would be stripped naked. He'd rather let the money rot in a hole in the ground than hand it over on a plate to the Ivans. He kept only about fifty dollars American, pushing the rest of the money and the Swiss passport in the name of Werner Linz into the hole after the gun. Breathing heavily, his face running with perspiration, he got up off his knees and sat heavily on the bench.

It was nearly eleven when the door opened. Linz jumped to his feet as the officer who had spoken to him earlier appeared. The guard gestured with the Schmeisser.

'*Kommen Sie schnell!*'

Linz came out and the soldier grasped his shoulder roughly, marching him in front of the desk. The room was blue with tobacco smoke. They had all been smoking the cigarettes he had brought back from Lisl's place, eating the chocolate he had put in the paper sack with them. For some reason it made him angry, so angry that tears of frustration came into his eyes. There was another officer in the room now; he had taken the chair behind the desk, while the first captain stood behind him and to one side. His deferential attitude indicated that the newcomer, who was also a captain, had some other special status. The new arrival saw the tears in Linz' eyes and frowned.

'You are sad?' he said, softly. 'You are upset over something?'

'No,' Linz said. 'No, it's the smoke, it's nothing.'

'I see,' the officer said. He had a long, thin face, reflective in repose. His eyes were hooded, heavy-lidded beneath jutting eyebrows that met above the bridge of the acquiline nose. He said nothing, as if waiting for Linz to say more. In the end, the silence got to the prisoner. He summoned all his courage, adopting something like a tone of surprised outrage, but deferential.

'Surely, sir, you have kept me here long enough,' he whined, angrily. 'Surely you . . . '

'Shut up!' the man behind the desk snapped.

'But sir,' Linz said, astonishment coming into his assumed tone, 'I'm just an ordinary worker. What can you want with me? Why . . . ?'

The officer got up and came around the desk, and Linz' voice tailed off.

'What is your name?' the officer said, gently.

'Heinrich Alton, s . . . '

His words were cut off by a brutal slap across the face, delivered quite unemotionally by the Russian with the back of his hand. Linz felt the salty sting of blood inside his mouth, and shook his head.

'Your name?'

'Heinrich . . . '

Again the punishing blow, this time delivered on the other side of the face. Linz felt his cheekbone throbbing, and his left eye was watering so badly that he could not see out of it.

'More tears?' said the silky voice. 'Again — who are you?'

'I have told you, sir,' Linz whined. 'I am . . . '

He flinched, expecting another blow to his face, but instead the Russian hit him very hard, very low in the belly. Linz went down on the dirty floor, retching, his breathing coming with difficulty, squirming around hunched over to contain the pain. The guard dragged him unceremoniously to his feet and at a gesture from the officer brought him in front of the desk, holding him upright.

'So,' the senior officer said. 'A stubborn one.' Then over his shoulder to the other one: 'It makes a change.' The second officer nodded, smiling coldly.

'All right,' the Russian said, nodding to the other guard. Linz watched him go into the room in which they had made him wait, a cold slimy hand seeming to claw his guts. The guard came out after a few minutes with the gun and the money and the passport. He put them on the desk in front of the officer and stood back. The Russian looked at Linz and smiled like a cat who has cut off the mouse's way back to the mousehole.

'Yes, my friend, we were watching you all the time,' he said. 'Now, for the last time, who are you, what is your name?'

Linz said nothing, for he was now truly afraid. As if sensing this, the Russian reached into the breast pocket of his uniform jacket and pulled out a small flat wallet of black leatherette. He flipped it open and laid it on the desk where Linz could see it. It was some kind of identity card, Linz realised, for the officer's photograph was on the right-hand side. Linz could not read what it said. The only thing he recognised was the hammer and sickle emblem.

'What is it?' he said hoarsely.

'*Narodnyi Kommissariat Vnutrennikh Del,*' the officer replied.

'I don't speak Russian.'

The officer made an exasperated sound of disbelief.

'NKVD,' he said. *Sicherheitspolizei.* Secret police.'

'Oh, sweet Jesus Christ,' Linz said in English.

11

Paris
25 July 1945

The man Sedillo knew as André sat in a grubby hotel room in the rue Durantin. It was very hot outside. Birds were singing, and he could hear a radio playing somewhere. A young woman with her hair in curlers was leaning on the railing of the balcony outside her apartment in the *maison meublée* across the street. She was about twenty-five, her mouth discontented and sulky. He pulled the curtains across.

Earlier, he had bought a bottle of white wine in the shop on the corner of the rue Tholozé and left it in the tiny sink with the cold tap running to cool it. Now he sipped some of the wine from a tumbler and looked at the weapon on the bed.

The old man had done a magnificent job, worth every peseta of the thousand dollars he had paid him. Working on the weapon lovingly, by hand, each stroke of the file carefully considered, Sedillo had adapted a gun of the type used by many rich people in Spain for clay-pigeon shooting, an over-and-under double-barrelled shotgun whose barrel he had cut down to about ten inches. The inside of the barrels had now been rifled to maximise accuracy over the short range which had been specified. The stock had been stripped and in its place Sedillo had provided a skeleton grip like the pistol grip on an assault rifle but with a stalk reaching from just behind the breech tailored to the exact $11\frac{7}{8}$ inches that would make the flat wooden butt plate fit snugly against the shoulder of the man who would use it. The gun, stripped, fitted neatly into the foot-long carrying holster which Sedillo had provided. A strap around the shoulder, and the whole thing would hang, comfortably, inside a man's jacket without showing any more than a slight bulge. After practising for three hours, the man in the hotel room had got his time for assembling the gun down to just under two minutes. When the time came, he would have it down to one. In a small cigar wallet with five fluted receptacles lined now with double thicknesses of velvet was the true evidence of Sedillo's genius. When they had tested the gun in the cellar of the old man's house on the calle de Segovia, overlooking the Campo del Moro, Sedillo had smiled at his companion's enthusiasm over the weapon and — more especially — the cartridges.

They were about as fat as good cigars, slightly shorter, with wide copper butts at the percussion end. The bullets were handcut from heavy rubber, blunt-ended, with just enough shape, Sedillo explained, to maintain their true trajectory across the short distance they would have to travel.

'The gun has no range at all with bullets of this kind,' he had said.

Then carefully, so as not to offend, 'You understand this?'

'I understand perfectly. But I have doubts about the efficiency of the thing.'

Sedillo had smiled and flicked on a

light in the galleried cellar. At one end there was a solid stone wall, lined with a soft steel plate, pitted with the scars of many bullets fired in testing and proofing by the old gunsmith. In front of it he had set up the target the younger man had described to him. It was a terracotta bust of some long-forgotten Roman, packed inside with clay until it weighed around ten pounds, the weight of the human head. A wooden block in the neck, which had been sawn through just below the chin, and another, heavier piece of wood nailed to the wooden bench on which the bust stood, were joined by a thick, solid metal spring taken from the suspension of an old Citroën in some obscure garage the old man knew.

'It may be a little strong in comparison with the real thing,' he had said. 'But test it, anyway.'

The results had been spectacular, much better than he had hoped. In addition, the explosion when the gun was fired was a dull, muffled sound, not the sharp crack he had anticipated.

'The muzzle velocity is lower,' Sedillo

explained. 'Only about 1000 feet a second. But it is enough, as you see.'

Now, in Paris, he was ready to begin.

He had read the file that Rafferty had given him over and over and over, impressing the vital statistics upon his formidable memory until he could recite them as if he had always known them. George Robinson Campion, Junior, son of rich parents, born in Spokane, Washington, 14 September 1885. The father an eccentric, cultured man with a mistrust of the near-frontier conditions in the local schools, who had taught his son to the age of twelve by reading to him daily from the classics and the Bible. At twelve, Campion had gone to private school and from there into West Point Military Academy, graduating in the class of 1909. As a second lieutenant, he had married a Virginia tobacco heiress, Patricia Arlen, and throughout his early career lived the life of a rich, upper-class military man with impeccable connections: aide to the Chief of Staff of the Army, rising rapidly through the echelons of rank — Captain, Major, Lieutenant-Colonel. Campion had served with distinction in the First World War, been decorated for gallantry right at the end (Distinguished Service Medal), and when it was over, returned to the leisurely life of the American Junker, playing polo (400 cups, 200 ribands) writing treatises on military history and science, serving in the United States and Hawaii until Pearl Harbour, when he was promoted Brigadier-General. His first command had been the invasion of North Africa in 1942, and he had controlled one mighty arm of the American forces in the Sicily invasion the following year. His reputation as a fighting general was quite enormous, his sweeping, daring thrusts into the territory dominated by his enemy legendary. Campion had been a major factor in the holding of the Bastogne salient during Hitler's last desperate Ardennes offensive, and had ended his war by being appointed Military Governor of Bavaria.

That was the official side of the story. There was another, and it had taken some time to put together. There were, even in wartime, enough people interested in the publications of their allies and their enemies for the neutral embassies to keep fairly comprehensive files of their newspapers and magazines. In the Swiss Consulate in Lisbon's Avenida dos Aliados he had spent long hours scanning their complete file of the New York *Times*, back issues of *Life* and *Time*. The library of the University of Göteborg in Sweden had yielded worthwhile material, including articles written by Campion for the old *Cavalry Journal*. And covertly, here and there, he had picked up army scuttlebutt from enlisted men and officers in bars, in restaurants, in clubs. Campion was a hated hero, an awesome legend. They called him 'The old bastard', 'Two-gun Pete', 'Bloodyguts' with reverent irreverence. His unstable nature was well known — one officer called him 'advanced manic-depressive'. There were tales of Campion's unabashed lobbying for decorations for his men — and for himself. There had been irrational outbursts which alienated the very people on whom he depended for support, bringing him many times to the verge of court-martial. Despite heavy drinking, the

135

man was a prude. Despite the profanity he was deeply religious. He was a man who had been witnessed pissing in the Rhine when he crossed it, and weeping when he underwent one of his frequent bouts of intense patriotism. The man who had one of the largest libraries on military history in the United States could also out-curse the foulest-mouthed Polish dogface in the foxholes. Everything about Campion was contradiction — and a feast for any amateur psychologist. Martinet, prude, glory-hunter, oaf — which was the real man, if any, or all? The shy, happily married Campion or the Campion who always made sure there were pretty Red Cross nurses around when he gave dinners for visiting brass?

The anecdote which revealed most about Campion was the one he had heard about what had happened at West Point during Campion's graduation year. During sharp-shooting exercises, the story went, Campion had deliberately stuck his head up into the line of fire, to see, as he later explained, 'how afraid he would be and to train himself not to be scared.'

The man in the hotel room in Paris lit a cigarette and leaned back on the sausage-shaped, rock-hard pillow.

Campion's travelling from his headquarters in Bavaria usually consisted of irregular trips into Munich and local commuting between the small towns scattered around the foothills of the Alps, dining with local dignitaries, making appearances on behalf of the United States, a kind of goodwill ambassador without the rank. Once a month he visited the SHAEF headquarters in Frankfurt. These visits, too, were irregular in the sense that although they were never less, never more than monthly, they were not to any pattern that he had been able to establish. To know where Campion would be, and when, in advance, it was going to be necessary to penetrate his staff. Ticking them off in his mind, the man on the bed discarded Campion's G2 in charge of intelligence, a middle-aged colonel named Oscar Cook who had been an economist in the Department of the Interior before the war. His cook was a Chinese, his driver a Private First Class.

Nothing there. His personal aide, and the best bet, was Lieutenant Colonel James French, but French was impeccable in his personal habits, a happily-married man with two children and a pretty wife in Saddle River, New Jersey, all of whom adored Campion. Unlikely, then. That left Campion's Signals Officer, in charge of all communications at the Military HQ in Bad Tölz: Colonel Elton F. Stewart. Stewart, too, was married and had two children, but he also had a German mistress. It was strictly against official orders and Campion's Victorian morality, but common camp gossip nonetheless. It was likely that everyone on Campion's staff but the General himself — and possibly his aide — knew of the liaison. The woman was Theresa von Rodeck, a thirty-five-year-old Austrian countess of noble birth who had been suspected of Nazi sympathies (it had never been proven) and whom Stewart kept in an apartment near the Officers' Club in Munich, a house near the old English Gardens where the bombing had been lightest. Stewart saw the woman at irregular intervals, his duties at Bad Tölz being dictated by Campion's equally irregular hours and moods.

Yes, the man on the bed thought. He swung his legs to the floor, and got up to pour some more wine into the tumbler. It was time for Shelley to reappear.

12

Istanbul
10 August 1945

It was the season when the wise man governs his temper and his tongue, the time when usually-docile animals bite or kick, faithful wives cheat, old friends plot betrayal. It was the season when the hot winds, the *lodos*, pant across the Sea of Marmara and stir the dust of every corner of every alley in the grimy, pestiferous shell of what was once New Rome, Byzantium.

The British Consulate at Beyoglu was a solid stone building, its discreet façade unremarkable, the windows shuttered against the relentless heat outside. There were few people on the streets. Those who had to bear the stultifying city heat were indoors, their fans or air conditioners on, cold drinks in beaded glasses at hand. Those luckier ones who could escape the city were lying on the wide empty beaches of the Bosphorus, their faces and bodies shaded with newspapers which carried screaming headlines announcing the dropping of the second atomic bomb on Nagasaki, predicting the imminent surrender of Japan and the end of the long, long war.

There had been drinks in the Ambassador's office the night before, a sort of muted celebration where pleasure at the ending of the war was mixed with unexpressed distaste for the means by which that ending had been achieved. What the real horror of Hiroshima and Nagasaki had been they did not, could not know. They only knew it had been more terrible than any other event in the history of war.

One man in the Consulate, however, felt no pity for the Japanese. Arthur Pottersman, Inquiry Officer at the Consulate, had been in Singapore in 1941, and he laid down the borrowed copy of yesterday's London *Times* nodding with satisfaction that the little yellow bastards had finally been given the kind of treatment they deserved. He got up from his desk, preparing to beetle off quietly to the Gents for a quick smoke, when a man came into the reception hall. He was short, stocky, dressed in an old-fashioned double-breasted suit with that peculiar Middle Eastern cut so apparent to European eyes. The man looked about him with the disoriented air that people have in a strange place where they do not know how to comport themselves, who to ask for assistance. He saw Pottersman and turned towards him.

'Yes, sir, can I help you?' Pottersman said, going to meet him.

'Please,' the man said. 'I will speak with Sir Charles Down.'

Pottersman was not normally given to sudden insights; he was a phlegmatic individual whose duties were a cross between doorman and security guard. Yet there was something about the visitor's demeanour which sent a small chill shivering across his spine. To his surprise he found his hands clammy, his legs trembling slightly. Good Lord, he thought. Good Lord.

'If you'll wait a moment, sir,' he said, 'I'll see if he's available.

'And your name?'

'No names,' the man said. He kept looking back at the door, Pottersman noticed. Good Lord, he thought. There was no question about that accent. The man was a Russian. And the service pistol Pottersman had never fired was in the drawer of the desk. He slid the drawer open as he picked up the phone with his left hand. He dialled and spoke into the phone, nodded and stood up.

'Will you come with me, please?' he said.

He ushered the man along the corridor to the office of the Acting Consul and knocked. Then he opened the door and showed the man in.

'How do you do,' the Acting Consul said to the visitor. 'Do sit down, please.' The Russian sat in the armchair facing Mr Page's desk, and Pottersman turned to go.

'Oh, Potters,' Mr Page said. 'Stay by the door, will you? Outside, there's a good fellow.'

When the door closed he turned to face his visitor.

'You are Sir Charles Down?' the man said.

'No, I am Harold Page, the Acting Consul,' Page told him. The man's face set into something like a sulk.

'I wish speak only Sir Charles Down,' he said. He looked uneasy, his eyes moving around, checking everything in the room as if it concealed hidden men with weapons.

'I have sent for him,' Page said, easily. 'He'll be here in about fifteen minutes. Perhaps you could tell me what it's about?'

'I am Volkov,' the man said. 'Konstantin Volkov.'

'Yes,' Page said encouragingly.

'I speak more later,' Volkov said and that was that. Despite several attempts, Page could not get anything further from the man until about ten minutes later Pottersman knocked and Sir Charles came into the room. He was not a tall man, but he bore himself very erect in a military fashion, his leonine head high.

With his faultlessly groomed iron-grey hair, his quietly elegant clothes and thin aesthete's face, he gave an impression of utter rectitude.

'I am Charles Down,' he said to the Russian, who had risen from his chair as he came in. 'I understand you wish to speak to me?'

'Yes, I wish,' Volkov said. 'But only you. Not him. Nobody else.'

'Very well,' Down said. 'Harold if you wouldn't mind leaving us alone?'

'Of course, sir,' Page said. A look from Down had been enough to tell him what to do now. As soon as the door closed behind him he hurried downstairs to the communications room, rattling out instructions to the Duty Officer. In a few scrambling moments of hasty work, jackplugs were pulled, switches set, tapes turning. Page picked up a pair of earphones and listened in to one of the speakers, the Duty Officer leaning his head over to hear in the other.

'Now,' they heard Down say, the leather chair squeaking as he sat down. They heard a click and the sigh of expelled breath as cigarettes were lit. 'What is it you wish to speak to me about?

'I am Volkov,' the man said. 'Russian Embassy. Consul for Istanbul since five months.'

'Yes,' Down said, lengthening the vowel.

'Really I am intelligence. Area director NKVD. You know NKVD?'

'Ah, yes,' Down said, nothing but interest and encouragement in his voice.

'You are my — what you call? Opposite number. Yes?' There was a silence, and then the listeners heard the Russian laugh, a short barking sound.

'So, you not speak. No important. I bring you something. How is it said when I wish make arrangement with you?'

'A proposition?'

'Yes. That. I have information. I sell to you.'

'I see,' Down said. 'What kind of information, Mr Volkov?'

'Ahah,' Volkov said. 'First we make prop . . . proposition.'

'You want money, I take it?' The Duty Officer grinned. Only an Englishman would have noticed the sneer in Sir Charles' voice. But he was doing it by the book, all the same. The main thing was to keep the contact alive, keep channels open until a specialist could take over — standard FO procedure. Sir Charles was no more responsible for intelligence than old Potters. They needed someone from PID for that.

'I give you list,' they heard Volkov say. They heard the rustle of paper being passed from the Russian to the diplomat.

'What exactly is this?' they heard Down say. 'I'm afraid I haven't my glasses with me.'

The listeners smiled. Good old Downers, Page thought. He knew they had to get it on the tape.

'Very good, then,' Volkov said. 'I read. What I bring, all these: addresses all buildings in Moscow of NKVD, details their alarm systems. If you also want, I can bring wax, wax . . . '

'Impressions?'

'Impressions of keys to these place. And guard schedules. Yes, and all NKVD automobile registration number — good, not? I bring you list of all Soviet agent operating in Turkey, and their contact codes.'

'Mr Volkov,' Down said, with just the right note of apathy in his voice.

'Wait, wait, more,' Volkov insisted, his tone becoming a shade more anxious, eager. Good work, Downers, Page thought.

'I bring names three Russian agents working in government in London. I have information about assassin of American OSS man in Munich — of officers in Germany who hired him. I have details of plot by former SS men to free Goering from Spandau. All these. I bring you all these thing.'

'I see,' Down said slowly. Page and the Duty Officer looked at each other.

If Volkov had half the information he was talking about, this was the biggest security break intelligence had had for years.

'I want money,' Volkov said. 'Thirty thousand English sterlings. British passport with false name. Transportation to Cyprus. All these.'

'Mr Volkov,' Down said, 'I must speak

with the Ambassador about what you have told me.'

'Yes,' Volkov said. 'Speak, please.'

The men in the basement heard Down tell Potters to come in and stay with Volkov while he saw the Ambassador.

'Under no circumstances is anyone to enter or leave until I return,' he said, and hurried up the corridor to the elevator which he took to the first-floor office of the Ambassador, Sir Arthur Handasyde Buchan. They spoke quietly for perhaps ten minutes. Down growing steadily more sullen, Buchan steadily less interested. Finally, he told Down to channel the whole thing through to London.

'I'm sorry, Charles,' he said. 'But I'm demmed if I'll have my Embassy turned into a spy nest for those Johnnies at PID. Hand it over to them or SIS in London. Wash your hands of it.'

'But, sir . . . ' Down began.

'Turn it over to the specialists, Charles. Please,' the Ambassador said smoothly, and then turned half aside to look over some papers on the right-hand extension of his huge mahogany desk. They were estimates for the new squash court at the Embassy in Ankara and, as usual in Turkey, they were going to cost him hours of haggling and headaches. Down was dismissed and he knew it; he went back downstairs, getting hold of his temper in the elevator, composed again as he came back into the room where the Russian sat waiting.

'I have spoken with the Ambassador,' he told Volkov. 'He agrees with me that we must await a decision from London. I must ask you to give me time to contact them.'

Page and the Duty Officer looked at each other with widening eyes. Surely they weren't going to let the Russian out of the Consulate? It was like catching a record salmon and then telling it to swim away, come back a little later.

'Is understood,' Volkov said. If he was perturbed by what Down had told him he did not show it. 'Now you will do certain things I tell you.'

'Yes,' Down said. 'Of course.'

'First, you and you only will send these information to London. They must be written in your hand only. No typewriting. I am believe there is a Russian agent in this Consulate or in your Embassy in Ankara.'

Down's eyebrows rose at this further revelation, but before he could ask the obvious question, Volkov continued. 'These information must not go to London by telegraph, because possibility of interception exists. You agree?'

'I agree,' Down said. 'I will send them by diplomatic pouch.'

'Today is 10 of August. I wait only until last day this month. If no reply from you by then, we make no further contact. Is agree again?'

'Certainly,' Down said. Then, artlessly: 'And if I need to contact you?'

'Not possible,' Volkov said flatly. He stood and extended his hand, European fashion. 'Goodnight, goodbye, comrade,' he said warmly.

Within minutes he was gone, and Down went back to his office at the rear of the building. They brought up the tapes and he locked himself in the room, working and reworking the brief for PID in which he outlined everything which had been said, the specific items about the Russian agents in London, the assassinated American officer, the SS plot to free Goering, his own assessment of the man and his conviction that it was not a 'plant' but that Volkov was a genuine defector with vital intelligence information. The Ambassador drafted a covering memo to Sir Stewart in London and the brief went into the diplomatic bag.

Twenty days later Down received a brief acknowledgement from London that his brief had been received and was being looked into, this despite several coded cables requesting urgent action in the interim. London seemed to be totally uninterested in the whole Volkov business. Sir Charles was properly disgusted although His Excellency the Ambassador remarked, not without some satisfaction in his voice, that those political intelligence Johnnies had probably decided that Volkov wasn't worth bothering with.

★　★　★

However, three weeks later, on the last day of August, they were to receive a signal from London that someone was being sent out to look into the Volkov business. At about two in the afternoon he would be ushered into Down's office, a calm unhurried chap of about thirty-five, wearing a dark blue tropical suit, a white shirt with a cutaway collar and a rather dashing cravat.

'Mr Philby, sir, from London.'

13

Bletchley Park, Buckinghamshire, England
14 August 1945

Charles Deverson sighed and turned away from the window.

There had been rain overnight and everything was a lovely, fresh summer green. The old cherry tree, long since stripped of its fruit by the ravenous blackbirds and wood-pigeons, shifted its leaves slightly in the faint breeze.

I must be getting old, he thought. He sighed again, the bright sunshine outside increasing his disinclination to return to the mass of paperwork on his desk, and brought back suddenly a memory of Alastair Denniston's children playing rounders on the lawn outside. He smiled mirthlessly. The lawn was long since gone, covered now with two-lane tracks for the vehicles which sped constantly between the sprawl of buildings that stretched in serried ranks across the slightly rolling grounds. There were over seven thousand people working at GCCS now: punch card operators, programmers, systems analysts — terminology which rang foreign to Deverson's ears, the necessary jargon of growth and progress.

It had been rather like a club in the early days of the war. They had wryly dubbed the place the 'Golf Club and Chess Society', an affectionate alternative to the forbidding 'Government Code and Cipher School' which was the establishment's official name. It had been arguably in those days (and was certainly now, he reflected) the most vital source of intelligence available to the British government, for it was here at Bletchley Park that all codebreaking, cryptanalysis, deciphering, and decoding of enemy signals had been effected.

He smiled, thinking back to the naïvete of the early days, the primitive machines, the guesses and stabs in the dark, the way the whole secret war in which they were engaged was really rather like an extension of doing the *Times* crossword; an infuriating puzzle which you always knew had a solution. It had been like a family then: university dons, linguists, political refugees, scientists, lexicographers, teachers of higher mathematics found by the gifted Denniston and brought here to struggle day and sometimes long into the night, pen and pencil, paper and mind against the fiendishly complex inventions of the German cryptographers. A game of wits played by two different kinds of fox. He smiled at his own analogy.

As the years of the war had gone inexorably by, so the sophistication of their own technique and that of the enemy had increased. To begin with, there had been simple enough guidelines, established many years before, during the First War. A cipher could use any letter of the alphabet as a substitute for another, transposing them, spelling the words backwards or in sections, scrambling them arbitrarily according to some predetermined plan or graph, even substituting numbers and symbols for letters. To that basic approach one added the refinements: secondary or even tertiary enciphering, multiple transposition, substitution or scrambling, or dummy letters ad infinitum. Against all this, the cryptanalyst had only his own intelligence and the knowledge that certain rules unfailingly applied.

Each language contains letters which occur more frequently in writing than others. In English they are e, t, a, i, o and r. In French they are e, a, i, s, t and n, and in German e, n, i, s, r, a, d and t. With the decision in 1944 to resume monitoring of Russian signals, extra linguistic specialisation had been necessary, but the basic rules still applied. The cryptanalyst prepared a 'frequency table' in which all the letters of the text were catalogued according to their frequency in the message. Then he applied all the tests he knew, all the existing tricks he had learned, all the guesses he could make, trying to penetrate the mind of the man or woman who had created the code he was trying to break.

The names they had thought up in those days, Deverson thought: Nihilist, Euclid, Gemini, Playfair, La Guillotine;

Dilly Knox and Oliver Strachey working all through the night on some particularly gruesome monster which wouldn't break. He remembered the excitement when the German sub U110 had been captured in May of 1941, all her codes and ciphers intact; and Bill Friedman's astonishing conquest of the German Enigma machine with its wired code-wheels that could pour out ciphers in a random profusion impossible to keep up with, let alone outstrip.

He remembered old George Travis, so much the absentminded professor that it wasn't even funny, pottering about in those musty old tweed jackets with the frayed leather cuffs and elbow patches, wandering off in the evening for a walk around St Mary's and then to the local for a half of bitter. These days he wouldn't be allowed off the place without a special pass, and the idea of taking a drink at the local was so far fetched that Deverson smiled at the thought of it. He sighed again and looked up at the huge room with its green metal desks and filing cabinets, the open-plan partitions which he so detested, heard the hum of activity, the shrilling of telephones, the constant chatter of the direct-line Telexes to the Admiralty, the War Office, and the Air Ministry. Men and women bustled about, folders under their arms, sheafs of signals in their hands, keeping the line of communications open between the Army, Naval and Air Force Sections into which operations at the Park were now divided, an industrious hive over which he, as Head of Section 37, now presided. Efficient, computerised, automated, cross-indexed, efficient and, for Deverson, completely soulless, Section 37 — named for the number of the building in which it was housed — was responsible for the interception of all messages between the Soviet Embassies and Consulates in the United States and the Russian intelligence complex at 19 Znamensky in Moscow — 'the Centre' as it was called in GCCS parlance.

I really must do some work, Deverson thought, slightly annoyed by his tendency to wool-gather — a trait he was noticing more in himself these days. He supposed it came from the realisation which had grown upon them all in these last few weeks that, far from seeing a decrease in the signal traffic they had been monitoring, the nearing of the war's end was bringing an increase which indicated that GCCS was extremely unlikely to be stepped down or even partially disbanded when hostilities ceased. He thought of Helen in the cottage at Salcombe, and fleetingly wished he could take out the dinghy for a few hours instead of . . . He sighed again, and turned his attention to the drafting of a memo he was preparing for the Permanent Under-Secretary (copy to Commander Travis, the Director, and to William Armstrong) on projected staff, requirements (1946) at Bletchley Park.

He had not completed more than half a paragraph when a discreet cough caused him to look up, slightly irritated.

'Yes, what is it?' What was the man's name? There were so many new faces these days, it was getting harder and harder to remember them all. Pearson, he thought, pleased with his memory.

'I'd like you to take a look at these, sir,' Pearson said.

He handed a sheaf of papers to Deverson, who frowned and put them down in front of him, spreading them out on the desk. He read the pencilled capitals with growing disbelief.

'Good God,' he said, softly.

Pearson smiled at his reaction but said nothing as Deverson scanned each of the signals, his breath becoming slightly shallower — the old excitement, he thought in one part of his brain, the same old excitement — an imperceptible tremor touching the tapered fingers.

'It's not a plant?' he said, knowing it couldn't be. Pearson shook his head vehemently.

'What's your assessment, then?' Deverson asked.

'We think it's a stupid, sir' Pearson said. 'A slip-up. Somebody in New York using the wrong code-book. It's a low-grade cipher — we broke it ages ago.'

'But this is top-level material,' Deverson said.

'I know that, sir,' Pearson said, with

just a shade of reproach in his voice.

Deverson smiled thinly, and asked another question.

'Nothing more, sir,' was the reply. 'They got on to it pretty quickly, and we're back to fragments now.'

'You have them ready?'

'About another hour, sir.'

Deverson nodded. 'Bring them to me immediately they are ready,' he said.

'Thank everyone for me, will you, Pearson. You've done well.'

'Thank you, sir,' Pearson said. Deverson's praise was rare. Lots of the staff of 37 said the old boy was past it, but Pearson thought there wasn't much old Dev missed, and he was gratified by Deverson's confirming reaction to the material he had brought in. He went back to his desk smiling, picking up the phone to let the boys downstairs know what Dev had said. And just wait until I tell Patsy tonight in the canteen, he thought, practising in his mind the precise way he would tell her of his coup.

Deverson sat staring at the meticulously transcribed messages for a long minute, and then he picked up the telephone, his voice decisive.

'Get me Commander Travis, immediately,' he said. 'Deverson, in 37.'

He waited a moment and then spoke again.

'Deverson here, sir,' he said. 'Can I see you right away? Yes, a matter of the greatest urgency.'

14

London
24 August 1945

In a large, sunny room on the seventh floor of the Government Communications Bureau in Broadway Buildings, almost directly opposite St James's Underground station, a top-level meeting was in progress. GCB was the nominal cover given to what was in fact the headquarters of the Special Intelligence Service, or MI6, as some people still preferred to call it. At the head of the highly-polished boardroom table sat the Permanent Under-Secretary of State for Foreign Affairs, an austere, grey-haired man in the top Civil Servant's uniform of black coat and striped trousers, highly starched white collar and grey silk tie. His eyes, grainy with lack of sleep, were cold and shrewd, the eyes of the professional who has seen many, many amateurs come and go.

On his left sat Major General Sir Stewart Menzies, Director of SIS, and on his right the Director of the Political Intelligence Division of the Foreign Office. Next to Menzies was Sir David Petrie, head of MI5, and opposite him, fingers plucking at the folder with its red Top Secret tab in the top right-hand corner, was Lord Swinton, Chairman of the National Security Executive.

'Perhaps you'd care to begin, Stewart,' the PUS said, 'since this matter seems primarily at least to fall within your province.'

'Hmph,' Menzies said. 'Hardly know what to make of it all, m'dear chap. Seems there's no argument, though, what?'

'Henry has already made it quite clear there's someone in the Washington Embassy leaking classified material to the Russians, Stewart,' Swinton said quietly. 'The question is: what is our best way of discovering who it is and sealing the leak?'

'Easy enough, I'd have thought, Phillip,' Menzies said. 'Put a good chap on to it. Beagle the blighter out, what?'

'There's rather more to it than that, surely,' the PUS said, lifting his chin urbanely at Petrie, while privately wondering when the PM was going to retire Menzies, who was patently past it.

'Our feeling exactly, Henry,' Petrie said. 'I'd like to take the items in your admirable dossier one by one, if I might, and perhaps postulate some courses of action we might take.'

Well done, David, Swinton thought. The PUS was glowing at Petrie's compliment: he was rather proud of his dossiers. The PUS looked at the man on his right, who nodded.

'Stewart?' he said. Menzies nodded, as did Swinton when the PUS lifted that aristocratic chin again.

'Taking the items in the order you have set them out, Henry,' Petrie began, 'it seems to me our field of action is fairly straightforward. The quality of the information — the fact that the telegrams from the PM to President Truman are transcribed down to the last detail, including the reference numbers — indicates that the leak is through someone with a fairly high security clearance, which means we can forget about clerks and secretaries. It has to be someone with access and opportunity, which means not less than attaché's rank.'

'Agreed,' the PUS said. 'Go on. David.'

'At the same time, the signals from Moscow asking for verification, for details of how the information was come by, suggest that perhaps they aren't altogether satisfied as to the reliability of the informant.'

'Good, good,' the PUS said. He liked a man who presented his thoughts precisely, after due deliberation. He wished there were more of them in intelligence.

'This indicates to me that we have to look for a man who may be more dependent upon the Russians than they are upon him. An unreliable man, but a man with enough security clearance to get access to this kind of information. He shouldn't be hard to find. But he'll be damned hard to get concrete evidence against. Which is why I would like to have permission to put the personnel of the

Washington Embassy under discreet surveillance.'

'Now, now, David,' Menzies put in quickly. 'Don't want a pack of bobbies thunderin' all around the place. I'm quite sure, if he exists, that my people can find the blackguard.'

'Are you suggesting, Stewart, that the Russian messages intercepted at Bletchley are not genuine?' the PUS asked, quietly.

Menzies spotted his blunder even as the PUS spoke, and hastened to repair his fences.

'Lord, no, Henry,' he huffed. 'Just sayin' I feel we can clean out our own stables, what?'

'I see,' the PUS said. Menzies slumped a little lower in his chair, and Petrie received a lift of the chin to proceed.

'I think that the majority of the other intercepts concern this meeting only to the extent that they are intelligence which may or may not be useful to us, whereas they may be of special importance to Bill Donovan or the FBI.'

'Your proposal?'

'That these signals go to the Russian

desk here at Broadway and also to Dick White at Ryder Street for information and action as necessary. At the same time they should be transmitted to the Directors of the FBI and OSS in Washington.'

'You might let Jim Angleton have sight of them as well, David,' Swinton put in. Angleton was an American working out at MI5 in charge of American Special Counter-Intelligence.

'Good idea,' the PUS said. 'I think we're all in agreement?'

'One thing,' said the Director of the Political Intelligence Division.

Every head in the room turned towards him, for it was the first time he had spoken since the meeting began two and a half hours earlier. PID was the central clearing house of all the intelligence organisations, its final word law to each of them. When its Director had an opinion to offer or information to impart, it was given from his unassailable position of overview which he had and his own personal, direct Cabinet sources.

'One thing,' he repeated, 'that should

be borne in mind apropos these American matters is that President Truman is contemplating the disbandment of the OSS, and replacing it with a very much scaled-down operation called the National Intelligence Authority.'

There were murmurs of surprise at his announcement.

'I'd heard one or two things on the grapevine, of course,' the PUS said, 'but I didn't know it had gone that far. What about Donovan?'

'He'll be released, and in due course will be given an ambassadorship. I would imagine,' the Director said with a faint smile, 'it will be in Southeast Asia somewhere.'

The listeners smiled at the considered subtlety of his understatement.

'Is there anyone in line to head the new Authority, Tony?' Swinton asked.

'I believe that a Rear Admiral Souers may be the first Director,' the PID man said. 'Of course, what he will be doing is establishing the nucleus of a new central intelligence authority, although with the present mood of America being towards massive, and rapid, disarmament and demobilisation, I shouldn't think Truman wants to announce it at this time.'

'Probably doesn't make all that much difference, anyway,' Menzies said, his face still sour at the rebuke he had received. 'We can only give them fragments, old chap. Just fragments.'

'You may be right, Stewart,' Petrie said. 'But nevertheless I think this information should be sent over. The request for details of FBI surveillance of Russian agents suggests that there may well be a leak in the Department of Justice, or even the FBI itself. I don't know who will follow up on the other thing — the OSS man killed in Munich. In fact I confess I'm puzzled that the Russians would be that interested in such a small matter.'

'Yet we've had two indications that they are,' the Director of PID said.

Once again all heads turned towards him. The man did come up with some surprises, Petrie thought.

'Two?' he said.

'Stewart's people have got a Russian in Istanbul who wants to come across,' the

171

Director said. 'He mentioned this Munich business, didn't he, Stewart?'

'I seem to recall something along those lines,' Menzies said. 'Of course, we were more interested in the other things he had to say.'

'Perhaps we should all hear about them?' the PUS said smoothly, knowing that Menzies would be reluctant to discuss SIS coups in front of Five and enjoying making him. One had little enough fun.

'I say, look here,' Menzies said. 'The Volkov thing's rather delicate, dontcherknow.'

'Just give us a brief rundown, Stewart,' said the Director of PID lazily.

'You needn't go into intimate detail.'

It was an order, for all its offhanded delivery, and Menzies ducked his head and told them about the Russian intelligence officer who wanted to come across, his Russian desk's suspicion that it might be a plant, the sort of information Volkov was offering being so good as to be too good, if they took his meaning.

'Nothing certain about friend Volkov at

all,' he finished. 'My people are checking him out now.'

'Good,' said the PUS. 'Then anything further you come up with on the American can be sent on to Washington. You'll bring this Volkov across, you think?'

'Sendin' one of my people out to look the situation over,' Menzies said.

'Soon as he can get away.'

The PUS nodded, and looked towards the man on his right. 'Tony?'

'Yes,' the PID man said. 'Let's get back to Homer.' Homer was the code-name of the man in Washington used in the Russian ciphers. 'I want him. I want him rather badly.'

'All things considered, Tony,' Menzies said, starting slowly, 'I'd like to get my people on to this. After all, Section Nine's rather closer to the whole Russian picture than any other department.'

The Director nodded, and looked at the PUS. One up for Stewart, his expressionless face said. He turned to Petrie. 'David?' he said, the faintest note of encouragement in his voice.

Petrie caught it and fielded beautifully.

'I think you're right, Henry,' he said. 'Section Nine is best equipped to monitor the Russian aspects. Let Stewart's people handle the Homer business. Five will merely keep a watching brief.'

'Good,' the PUS said, noting Menzies' scowl but ignoring it. Everyone in the room realised that while nominally SIS had charge of the matter, Petrie was still free to watch the watchers. He saw the faint smile touching the lips of the man on his right: good, that was what PID wanted, too.

'Well, then,' he said. 'Can we get all this into a formal resolution I can show to my minister?'

There was a murmur of agreement, and the PUS pulled a quire of feint-ruled foolscap paper towards him, unscrewing the top of his fountain pen and looking up.

'Resolved,' he said, writing. 'That SIS (Section Nine) will instigate — no, thoroughly investigate, yes, thoroughly investigate all aspects of security pertaining to the Washington Embassy and with specific concern, no, and especially concerning the man — or woman? — yes, or woman, code-named Homer. Stewart, you'll open a Double O file on this, of course.'

'Of course,' Menzies said, slightly offended at the suggestion that he needed to be reminded to do so.

'Good, good,' crooned the PUS, still writing. 'Copies to Tony, Philip and myself, I think.' he looked up to see if Petrie would rise, but the MI5 man knew better and held his peace.

'In the other security matters raised by the intercepts discussed at this meeting, it was resolved that the information should be passed to . . . Tony?'

'I think we can safely say to the Directors of the FBI and OSS and leave it at that for the moment, Henry,' the man on his right said.

'I'll be off to Washington in a few days, and be able to talk to the right man on the spot.'

'Excellent,' the PUS said. 'I'll draft a memorandum this evening.

'The Minister shall have it tomorrow. Copies to you all, of course. Sherry?'

He pressed a button under the table and after a few moments, in which cigars were lit, a decanter of sherry and glasses were brought in by a commissionaire and placed on the table. Petrie stood to pour the drinks, but the PUS waved him back to his seat, doing the honours himself.

'Tony,' Swinton was saying, 'I'd like to hear more about this step-down of the OSS you were talking about. What do you know about this Souers chap?'

'Damned little, frankly,' the Director said, sipping the sherry, then putting it down. They really had the most abominable amontillado at 54 Broadway. Probably because they were all whisky drinkers, taste buds burned away years ago, he thought. 'That's why I'm off to Gossip City.'

Menzies looked at his watch, pointedly, and the PUS caught the hint.

'Have we any other business, gentlemen?' he asked. 'David, perhaps you'd be so kind as to collect the dossiers?'

As Petrie went around the table and picked up the folders, they got up, leaving the room one by one, footsteps echoing down the stone corridors with their ugly tiling and government green and cream plastering. The Director of the PID was the last to leave. He came out into the street, where his Humber drew discreetly to the kerb. He looked up at the sky thinking, it looks as if it might rain.

'Looks as if it might rain,' he said to the driver as he got into the car.

'Do the gardens good, sir,' the driver said. He looked over his shoulder, waiting for instructions.

'The club, I think,' the man in the back seat said.

The driver nodded and released the handbrake, heading smoothly into Tothill Street. His passenger remained silent in the back of the car as they headed through the traffic in Parliament Square, his mind still going over the things which had been discussed at the meeting he had just left.

All in all, he reflected, it was probably judicious to have given Petrie the wink to keep an eye on the SIS people, while at the same time allowing Menzies such time as he needed to — what was the phrase he'd used? — clean his own stables. Incredible thing to say. Nevertheless, what was of paramount importance was that the person the Russians referred to as Homer should be quickly exposed and dealt with. Well, perhaps he could poke around a little himself when he got to Washington. And there was no question that Menzies or Petrie or both would come up with some answers soon enough.

There was, of course, no way for him to know that in fact it would be another six long years before the identity of Homer was revealed to be Guy Burgess, and even longer until SIS realised that the Head of Section Five, currently being sent by Menzies to Istanbul to look into the Volkov business, was a double agent named Kim Philby who had already betrayed Volkov to his Russian masters and was even now warning Homer that he was in danger. While Sir Charles Down fumed at the delays in Istanbul, arrangements were already being made in Moscow to ensure that Russia's growing interest in the death of Rafferty would remain effectively concealed from those investigating it for a considerable time to come.

Perhaps it was just as well that he knew none of these things as he looked forward now to the cheerful camaraderie around the bar in White's. The car turned into St James's Street, and the driver licked his lips. He just fancied a cold beer and there was a nice pub just around the corner in Jermyn Street. Lovely, he thought.

15

Munich
6 September 1945

Theresa von Rodeck rose at her customary hour, eight thirty. She ran a bath, luxuriating in the soft water and the perfumed bath salts which Elli had brought her a few evenings ago. He was sweet sometimes. She noticed a dull bruise, the size of a half-dollar, on the inside of her thigh and she frowned, the high-cheekboned face turning ugly in the unshaded overhead light of the bathroom. Then she pulled the plug and let the warm water out, turning the cold on full as she did. Crouching near the taps, she splashed her body and legs with the cold water, gasping and spluttering, her skin goose-pimpling like a sudden rash. Then she rose and stepped dripping wet and naked on to the beige wool rug by the side of the bath, reaching for the soft towel hanging behind the door. She had a slim, seal-like body with hardly any pubic hair. Her small breasts were firm and hard, her skin was taut with the cold water douching she had given herself, and she examined her body coldly, professionally, in the full-length mirror behind the bathroom door. She nodded, full lower lip sticking out a little. The signs were there for her own unforgiving eyes to see, the first tell-tale marks: the dimpling on the inner part of her thighs, the slight sagging of the buttocks, the flesh around the waist, and the beginnings of chickenflesh at the throat and between the small breasts. *Ach*, she thought, what can you expect, at thirty-five? She pulled tongues at herself in the mirror and donned a soft towelling robe, walking barefoot into the carpeted living room, pulling back the heavy curtains to let in the daylight. She grimaced at the bright sun and went into the bedroom, sitting in front of her mirror on the dressing table and looking at her reflection without really seeing it.

The things one had to go through to get a place like this. It was nice, though.

By today's standards, impossible luxury; only obtainable because of Elli, through the American know-how system — and so . . . one didn't mind it too much, being with the American. He was not too demanding, and there was always plenty of time for Reinhard. A slow, sexual smile touched her wide mouth. She was not a beautiful woman, Theresa von Rodeck, but there was about her a subtle emanation, a way of standing or something around the eyes and mouth that told men she would be good, very good, and once they had been alone with her for any length of time, they no longer saw that the nose was too short, too snubbed, that the high cheekbones gave her face an imbalance that was well away from beauty. They saw only the wide brown eyes, the beautifully shining helmet of dark hair, the mobile lips and the underlying promise of complicity. Theresa was proud of her sexual skills — God knew they'd been learned the hard way — and the power that what her body had, her eyes held, gave her over men. It had been a long road, though, the road to this apartment on the Lerchenfeldstrasse with its view across the old English Garden, its once-pristine lawns scarred now with bomb craters and the hastily dug trenches of the *Jugend*. She shook her head, tossing the long tresses: she would not think of that today. She would think of Reinhard, Reinhard's weight crushing her, Reinhard's strong hard young body on her, his hands touching her, rigid inside her. Her breath became shallower, her lips parted. She touched herself, her head going back slightly. *Ach, du*, she thought. Then she caught sight of her flushed face in the mirror and thought, no, my girl, none of that today. Not with Elli coming at eleven. She smiled at the *double entendre*, concentrating upon brushing her hair, one hundred long sweeping strokes with the hard brush every morning and every night. Men noticed your hair. Reinhard loved to run his hands through it, bury his face in it as he loved her. Reinhard whom she loved, foolishly, for he was only twenty-eight. She grimaced. I won't think about that, either. Reinhard knew about the American, of course. That was how she knew he loved her. With so many other women to choose from, those blue eyes and that tight, curling corn-yellow hair, he could have any of the hundreds on the streets who would happily give themselves to anyone who looked like Reinhard and had money as well. Reinhard didn't mind about the American, he knew it was the only way they could have this place. Sometimes he asked her about Elli, but she told him the truth, it was awful with him, she always thought about Reinhard while the American was doing it, loving him in her mind. And Reinhard would kiss her and call her his darling and they would make love and Elli would be forgotten until the next time.

He would be here in an hour or so, she realised, looking at her watch. Nine fifteen, my God, where does the time go? She wondered what he would bring today. He always came loaded with gifts: soap and chocolate, biscuits — what did he call them, cookies? — sometimes a pair of stockings, always cigarettes, cartons of them: Camel and Lucky Strike and

184

Chesterfield. Sometimes he wondered how she got through so much stuff and she would laugh lightly and say, darling, I'm a kept woman, remember? A kept woman is supposed to be extravagant. And he would laugh.

If only he made love properly it would be bearable, she thought. But in bed he was a pig. Like most Americans, he already had a fat belly that bulged over his belt. His body was thick, unattractive, matted with dark hair so that she had to close her eyes while he undressed, not to see him scrambling out of his uniform, not to see his hands trembling as he reached for her. Her eyes shut tight, she whispered endearments, forcing herself to imagine it was Reinhard, her speech coarsening, her invitations more basic, while the American pounded against her. He would snort and grunt, and he smelled as they all did of talcum powder, working at her as if he was breaking rocks until he groaned somewhere deep in his throat, emptying himself into her without caring that he had hardly aroused her, that she was up high but not over.

Afterwards he would roll away, patting her bare bottom like some doting parent patting the head of a clever little girl who has said something cute. Then he would be asleep within minutes, snoring lightly, and she would leave him there for an hour.

When he woke up he would take a bath — he was meticulous about it, washing his crotch like a penance — and they would sit and talk, drinking some wine or whisky, whatever he had brought. Talk about what was happening up at HQ, the stupid American soldier politics, that crazy fool Campion who was hiring all the ex-Nazis for his staff up at Bad Tölz, the other officers. He never took her out anywhere. Apart from Campion's puritanical feelings about sex, particularly illicit sex, fraternisation was taboo. He was breaking military law just by seeing her — she was supposed to be grateful instead of being bored, bored, bored. But never by so much as a change of expression did she let him know her thoughts. He was something you had to accept: like the shattered streets, the queues for bread, the thieves and derelicts in the broken buildings — the outside. She shuddered. She was never again going to sink to that. She had the apartment, well stocked with food by Elli, who gave her money, looked after the necessities of life. Reinhard was her own affair, nothing to do with the American. Anyway, he was married himself, so she had every reason. One night she had looked in his wallet and found snapshots of the wife, typical American, those fine white teeth, straight blonde hair done in a pageboy bob, standing outside a white frame house squinting slightly into the sun, laughing, secure in the safe world she lived in with the two little girls standing beside her, Molly and Melinda. They would never know what one had to do in a country like Germany, the things she had learned to do by the time she was eighteen, married off by her parents to Klaus von Rodeck *and it came back to her, suddenly, all of it, the glass-topped table with him lying beneath it, his face staring at her, into her, crouching on the glass topped table and doing it, doing it on him*. She wouldn't think about that today, either, thank you, or his friends in the years that followed, the black *Schutzstaffel* uniforms, the parties, the epicene things she had at first recoiled from, then slowly learned, slowly and painfully learned, patient as a wounded animal as she learned how to use the knowledge that her body gave her.

She sighed and got up from the dressing table, pouring water into the percolator and spooning coffee into the aluminium basket. One day we'll have enough money, Reinhard and I, she thought. One day the Americans will all be gone, and there'll be our little photography studio, maybe we'll sell cameras, they'll make cameras again one day.

The knock on the door was peremptory and loud, shattering her dreamy reverie. She frowned: it was too early for Elli. She went to the window. No jeep outside. It wouldn't be Reinhard, he knew the American was coming this morning. There was another knock and she went across the room to the door, standing with her ear against the wood.

'*Ja?*' she said loudly. One never knew who might come to the house these days.

'*Von Rodeck?*' A man's voice muffled by the door.

'*Ja.*'

'*Botschaft aus Bad Tölz für Sie.*'

A message? It must be from Elli, she thought, pulling back the bolt and turning the latch. The man in the hall was tall and dark-haired. She could not see him too well: there was no light in the corridor.

'Yes?' she said.

'I would like to talk with you, Fräulein,' the man said. 'On a matter of some importance.'

'I thought you said . . . ' Her eyes narrowed, and she made to slam the door, frightened. It could be police, the American military authorities, anyone. One never knew these days. The man stopped her. Without seeming to use any strength at all, he placed his hand flat against the door and she could not close it, although she tried.

'Who . . . who are you?' she panted.

189

'I'll come to that,' he said, pushing the door back open and coming into the room. Theresa von Rodeck made a run towards the telephone on the table. Elli had insisted she have it, although it was an astonishing luxury. The man did not try to stop her, but as she lifted the receiver he held up a photograph and let her see it.

'Before you do anything hasty,' he said. Her face went stark white and she put the phone down very gently, as if it might break. She had trouble speaking.

'Who are you?' she said again. 'Where did you get . . . that?'

The man smiled. Now that he was in the room she could see he had cold, blue eyes and an almost handsome, angular face. His hands were well kept, his clothes ordinary but of decent quality. He looked like someone who might be of middle rank in the government. His German was unaccented, the German of a foreigner who spoke the language perfectly but had not learned it in Germany where he would have picked up dialectic intonations.

'My name is Shelley,' he said, 'and don't worry. I'm not a policeman.'

'Thank God,' The words came out before she could stop them. She bit her lip and looked at the photograph. He held it out and she took it, staring at her own face smiling back among the crowd of sterner faces and the black uniforms.

'Where . . . where did you get this?' she managed.

'Rather more to the point,' the man said, 'is what I might do with it. Or these others.' He fanned them out on the table near the door: four of them. 'Rather good — you look very happy, very much at home,' he said. 'Now if I were to show them to Colonel Stewart, for example . . . ?'

'You . . . you wouldn't. You couldn't do that! Anyway, he wouldn't believe you.' Her head came up. She was getting control of herself, the panic subsiding. If he wasn't from the police, it must be something else — money. Her lip curled. Some of them would do anything for money.

'In fact,' she said, 'they may even be faked for all I know.'

'You know better than that, Theresa,' the man said gently.

'Well,' she said, tossing her hair back from her face, 'maybe. They might cause me a little embarrassment, I agree.' She pasted a tremulous smile on her face.

'I might . . . I might be able to get a little money, if that's what you . . . '

'No, no, Theresa,' he said, and for a moment his voice sounded exactly like Klaus's voice had sounded all those years ago, when he had told her to do something, something special for him and she had faltered, or done it wrong and he had punished her *oh, God, that riding whip*. She shuddered, looking at him with empty, beseeching eyes.

'What do you want?' she whispered.

'I want you to do something for me,' he said. 'Something very simple. If you do it well, these photographs of you with Doctor Goebbels will disappear and no one will even know they existed. If you do not, they will be sent to General Campion at Bad Tölz with a letter detailing your liaison with his Communications Officer, and . . . ' he waved a hand at the apartment ' . . . all this.' Her mind was racing as he spoke, trying to consider the implications, the alternatives. If only she could talk to Reinhard! If only there was some way to get the photographs away from this man, this Shelley. She saw his eyes on her, and realised that the towelling robe had fallen open when she ran towards the telephone. Of course! What a fool she was to forget the oldest weapon in her armoury! She let her lips part slightly, raising her breasts so that the robe fell further apart. He watched her and she thought she caught a gleam of heat in his eyes.

'I must think,' she said. 'Please, can't we talk about this?'

'If you like,' he said. 'But — '

'No, no,' she said. 'Please, won't you sit down? A drink, perhaps? Yes, a drink. I'd like one myself. Scotch? Cognac?'

'Scotch will do,' he said. He sat down on the sofa and leaned back while she poured two drinks with shaking hands. She brought them across to the sofa and sat beside him, not too close, she thought, tucking her legs beneath her, widening her eyes and looking at him over the rim of the glass.

'*Prost!*' she said and drank the fiery liquid, coughing a little as it burned her throat. He patted her back, and she smiled beneath the curtain of her hair. Touch, it was important that he had touched her.

'Thank you,' she said. 'Oh, that stuff is strong.' She was close to him now, and he could smell the perfume of the bath salts, the clean animal presence of her.

'Must you,' she said, her voice small, 'must you be so hard on me?' She let her hand fall on his forearm, looking into the pale eyes. She shifted her body slightly, just enough so that it seemed almost accidental, enough so that her thigh lay against his.

'It could be . . . very nice,' she said. 'If you wished.'

She looked down, lowering her eyes, the confused maiden making the hesitant approach, her voice timorous. Then she slowly lifted her head, parting her lips, the dark hair swinging back from her face, the long neck ready to go limp, and she saw the pale eyes burn into hers and his lips came down to meet hers, his mouth demanding, strong, hot. She felt the thrill of triumph melt into a deeper, stronger urge, God he was strong, his arms were like steel sheathed in shifting velvet, going around her and under her, lifting her from the sofa and carrying her towards the bedroom. She lay languid on the black sheets in the brass bed, the robe open, her body eager now, waiting for him, that winey taste of anticipated delight in her mouth mixed with the deeper glow of supremacy, the man looming above her. She closed her eyes and he descended upon her, taking her ruthlessly.

Then later, when she came back into herself and looked again with clearing eyes at the cracked ceiling above the bed, turned her head to see him, he was already propped up one one elbow, looking at her. There was a small smile on his lips, and she touched his mouth with her forefinger, tracing a line down across the firm chin and then down the throat, the centre line of the chest, her fingernail making a faint hissing scratching sound. Her whole body was tingling, soft. She had forgotten the time until she looked at the little watch on her wrist and saw it was almost ten thirty. God, Elli! She controlled her impulse to sit up, to panic; and instead rolled her breasts across his naked middle, reaching for the cigarettes on the bedside table, making a small sound in her throat as she writhed against his maleness.

'You,' she said, sitting up in the bed, lighting a cigarette and blowing the smoke at him. 'To frighten me like that. If only you'd said . . . '

Shelley didn't answer; he smiled at her and she felt a faint touch of unease.

'Wasn't it good for you, my darling?' she said, putting her hand on him. 'There, there. There. Ah, you see. So ready to begin again.' She bent over, nuzzling at him, and as she lay there, her hair spread like a fan across his naked thighs, her mind was sharp again and she knew that it must be now.

'Ah, my dear,' she said rolling over on her back, her face smiling up at him, 'It is so good. I'm so happy.'

'Are you?' he said.

'Yes,' she said. 'Because now I know you were only using those horrid photographs to scare me. I know you wouldn't do what you said, not after this.' She turned her head to the right to kiss him, making small sounds of kittenish pleasure. 'You'll give the photos to me now, won't you, darling?' she said.

'Of course,' he said. 'Eventually.'

She sat up abruptly, snatching the hair that fell across her face away with an angry hand.

'What do you mean, eventually?' she said, every trace of the kittenishness falling away.

'As I told you, my dear, there is something I want you to do for me.'

She was off the bed in one bound, her face knitting into squalling fury, and for the next few minutes she called him every filthy thing she had ever heard, pacing up and down, screaming at the unperturbed man who lay naked on the bed, calmly smoking the cigarette he had lit.

'And I thought you enjoyed it, too,' he said, reproachfully.

That started her off again, but she was rapidly running out of breath, her anger tailing off as she realised that it was having not the slightest impression upon him. This knowledge brought her failing anger back to full boil and she launched herself at him, hands clawed like talons, fingernails going instinctively for the emotionless eyes. He caught her arms as she came at him, screaming wordless curses, spittle flecking her writhing lips.

'Get out, get out, get out, get out, get out!' she shouted, struggling to free the hands locked in his larger, stronger ones. 'Get out of here!'

'Quietly, little one,' he said. He got up off the bed naked, still holding her arms, and then released one hand, his own right hand moving to the point where her neck swelled softly into her shoulder. The pain when he took hold of her there was so stunning, so atrocious, that she could not even scream. She went to her knees, mouth gaping like a landed fish, her eyes rolling up towards him in a wordless plea. His face was like something carved in stone.

'Now listen, bitch;' he said. 'And I will tell you what you are going to do.'

16

Rear Admiral Sidney Souers was in a quandary.

The preceding week, President Truman had officially disbanded the Office of Strategic Services and made arrangements for its Director, General Donovan, to take an extended and well-earned leave with 'the grateful thanks of the nation' before taking up his next appointment, a goodwill tour of Southeast Asia preceding his appointment as Ambassador to Siam. The wheels had been in motion for some time. Truman had already delegated three senior Cabinet members to form a holding organisation called the National Intelligence Authority, its job to wind down OSS.

'Get rid of the Martini set and the hangers-on,' was how Truman had put it, 'and put the others on ice for a while,' The NIA's main job was to report in committee to the Senate upon existing commitments and expenditures, so that the President could decide which of these activities should be maintained, and which terminated. The FBI was once more put in charge of all internal security, and Souers had been appointed Director of the NIA's executive arm, overseeing all military intelligence. Quite frankly, he wished he was back at sea.

Which, he had to admit ruefully, he hadn't been in quite a while. Most of the war he had spent on the staff of the Director of Naval Intelligence. It was that experience which had led, on Secretary Forrestal's recommendation, to Truman appointing him Director of NIA. Now he sat alone in the command office they had given him on the fourth floor of the Department of Justice building, wondering how the hell to begin making any sense out of the heaps of folders, piles of documents, bundles of books, reams of memoranda, accounts, appropriations forms and reports which covered OSS' activities as they presently existed in the field. He had, they had told him, until next February when the Senate appropriations committee met. At that time they were going to want at least an informed assessment of present and future commitments. And Souers was to do his damnedest to make sure they got it, in simple black and white, ABC terminology.

At least, that had been his intention when he started. But the pile of stuff on his desk (and the equally large pile of stuff on the desks of the three assistants he had been given) stared back at him to prove how naïve his original intentions had been. There were around six hundred 'open' files in all, covering activities where no black and white, ABC terminology was possible. Souers was rapidly getting the feeling that everything OSS had been involved in had been tinted a special kind of grey: whether it was the Balkans or Burma, China or Hungary.

Then on top of all this was the ongoing flow of intelligence information which he was supposed to evaluate and then pass to the appropriate body: DNI, FBI, Army Intelligence, and all the rest.

He shrugged, turning the air conditioner down to reduce the droning whine which the dictaphone picked up and immediately feeling the muggy warmth leech the sweat from his body. He took off his jacket and pulled the dictaphone across, hewing back to the simple system he had devised. All the files had been separated into piles according to the date upon which the action had originated. He was working backwards from the most recent, reading the files carefully and then dictating into the machine instructions which would be followed up by his assistants. Have to ask for more help soon, he thought.

By nine o'clock he had read eighteen files, making meticulous notes for follow-up the next morning. He looked at his watch. Too late for dinner: it was going to be another hamburger on the way back to the apartment. He thought of Nancy in the house at the Vineyard, and wondered whether to call her. Later, maybe, in the apartment, he thought.

He shifted his attention to the pile of material on his left. These were dossiers which his staff had already looked out in connection with earlier notes he had made on the dictaphone, cabled replies from inquiries made, signals from British intelligence and from agents overseas containing information NIA had requested. He opened the first one. It was the OSS internal dossier on Colonel James Rafferty. Rafferty, he thought, Rafferty? Then his conversation a week or so previously with the quietly spoken Britisher who had come to his office came back to him. There had been some Russian interest in the fact that Rafferty had been murdered in an apartment in Munich. He had decided it was worth checking to see why. Clipped to the personnel folder was a file from Army CID with the bare details of their fruitless investigation into the murder. Rafferty had been on leave in Munich (strange place to go for a vacation, Souers thought) and staying in an apartment (not the Officers' Club?) when he had been shot by an unknown assailant using a German paratroop rifle.

There were some clinical details of Rafferty's wounds. The contents of his pockets and baggage, such as they were, had been forwarded with the report. There was a meticulous list of the contents, nothing special about them. Souers supposed they had been sent to Army CID and from there to Rafferty's next of kin. Watch, wallet, diary, dogtags, penknife, cigarette case (how pathetic the paltry trinkets a man carried all his life seemed when they were listed like this on an impersonal buff army report), clothing, money — eight hundred dollars, Souers thought, surprised, a lot of cash to be carrying. A cellophane envelope was attached to the report, containing photostats of the papers found on Rafferty. Photographs, features hard to distinguish in the negative copies. A woman, standing by a tree. He looked at the personnel file. No wife. A sweetheart, then. A receipt from a restaurant in Naples. Naples? He checked the CID report again. Vacation in Munich, he read. What had Rafferty been doing in Naples? Souers sifted through the other papers until he came to the photostat of the travel orders Rafferty had been carrying. Yes, he had come to Munich on a Transport Command flight from Naples. The travel orders were given an AAA rating, which meant Rafferty had gotten top clearance from someone. For a vacation? He looked again at the papers. They had been authorised out of SHAEF in Frankfurt. Had Rafferty given out the vacation story as a cover? Had he been on an assignment somewhere — with Naples as his real destination, Munich as his cover? And killed in Munich for — what? Why were the Russian intelligence people asking for information on his death? What was their interest in the man? Rafferty — he checked the file again — was at the time of his death Assistant Commander, European theatre of operations. Privy to high-level, but not a great deal of top secret, intelligence material, and certainly not policy documents. He picked up the telephone and dialled a number. It was answered on the second buzz.

'Clyde,' he said. 'Sidney. You boys work late over there.'

'We never sleep,' came the sardonic reply. 'What can I do for you, Sid?'

'I want a rundown on something and I want it chop chop chop,' Souers said.

'Can you help me out?'

'Shoot.'

'If I wanted to check on the movements of one OSS officer, back in — wait a minute — May, June, around there, how would I go about it?'

'In Washington, you mean?'

'First, yes,' Souers said. 'Then any movement out of town — out of the country, even.'

'You know where?'

'No, that's what I want to find out.'

'Well . . . if he used official transportation, you can probably get it from the requisition slips. Every vehicle that's requisitioned has to turn in a slip at Transport HQ showing where he went, how many miles — so he can get his gas ration. That's if your man used official transport. From what you've said so far, I'd guess he might have stuck to cabs.'

'Are you kidding?' Souers said. 'In this town?'

'You may be right,' Clyde said. 'May or June, you said?'

'Better make that from the first of May through June,' Souers replied.

'Thanks a bundle,' was the dry retort. 'How soon you want this?'

'How soon can I have it?'

'Take three or four hours,' he was told. 'Minimum.'

'Get at it,' Souers said, and started to give him the details from the file on the desk in front of him.

'I'll wait at this number,' he said, when he had finished. 'Call me back. It's top priority.'

'Oh, Christ, why didn't you say so?' Clyde said. 'Stay there. I'll get back to you within the hour.'

He rang off, and Souers returned to the papers on his desk, rubbing his stinging eyes and smoking cigarette after cigarette until his mouth tasted like a compost heap. He sent a night man along to the machine in the corridor for some coffee, not wanting to leave the phone or the file he was reading and rereading, getting to know all he could about Michael Rafferty, the excitement building in him. The Britisher who'd visited him had also talked of an intercept they had made which indicated that there was a leak somewhere in the Justice Department, through which the Russians had been getting information. OSS wasn't the Justice Department, but it was near enough. Had Rafferty been the link? Was that why he had been killed? Was that why the Russians wanted to know about it? Had he been taken out by his own people? If so, why was there no record of it? He had seen some of those files with the brutal red block letters stamped diagonally across the page: *Terminate with extreme prejudice*. There was nothing in Rafferty's file. Nothing. He lit another cigarette, exclaiming with disgust as he realised he had done it, but puffing on the thing nevertheless. He sat back in the chair and let his mind open up, considering possibilities, discarding them, adding up, taking away, being left always with an unlikely hypothesis. Come on, Clyde, he thought, glaring at the telephone. As if on command, the telephone rang, making him jump. He snatched the receiver off the hook.

'Souers,' he said.

'Sid, it's Clyde. We lucked out. He used official cars. Got your pencil handy?'

Souers looked at the words he was writing, a deep crease of puzzlement growing between his heavy eyebrows. It made no sense at all, none at all. The voice on the other end stopped talking, and he stared at the paper.

'Sid, you still there?' the voice squawked.

'Uh? oh. Yes, sorry. Sorry, Clyde.'

'Tell you what you want to know?'

'I don't know yet,' he said. 'I don't know.'

'He sure as hell got around, that Colonel,' Clyde said, and Souers could hear him smiling. 'Goodnight Sidney.'

'G'night Clyde. And thanks. Thanks a lot.'

'Any time,' Clyde said and hung up.

Rear Admiral Sidney Souers sat and stared at the words he had written on the paper in front of him. *National Airport 23 May connect with flight Toronto 0930 hrs. National Airport 29 May connect with flight New York 0820 hrs. National Airport 2 June connect with flight New York 0820 hrs.* Souers checked the receipt from the restaurant in Naples again. It was hard to read, but it looked like 5.6. 6 May? That wasn't possible. Then he remembered the European way of writing the date was the opposite of the American. 5.6 was 5 June. Seventeen days later Rafferty had been shot dead in Munich. What had he been doing in the intervening period? He looked at his watch, realising with a shock that it was almost one o'clock. He took a deep breath and lit another cigarette, crumpling the day's third pack and throwing it into the dustbin. He hesitated several minutes before growling 'dammit!' beneath his breath. Then he picked up his telephone and dialled a number. A sleepy voice replied. 'Souers, National Intelligence Authority,' he said. 'I want to speak to the Chief of Staff. Yes, I *know* what time it is.' He listened to the voice at the other end for a moment, then his patience ended. 'Lady,' he said, levelly. 'If you don't want to be the most unemployable woman in

211

the city of Washington, you'd better put me through. And I mean *instantly!*' There was a venom in the way he spoke the last word that made the telephonist jump, startling the girl next to her at the switchboard.

'Yes, *sir,*' she said, and put him through.

17

Michael Rafferty's parents were kindly old folks who lived in a big rambling frame house on the corner of Garland Avenue, looking out from the bluff on which the house stood across Ninth and the sprawl of downtown LA. The little Stars and Stripes was still hanging in the window, almost as though Rafferty's parents hadn't yet accepted the fact of their son's death.

They were more than happy to help Green in any way they could: and talked about Mike, and his boyhood pranks, as if he were due to come back into the house any time. They showed him the dormer room Rafferty had always used when he came home ('wasn't too much of the time these last few years,' the old man said) and left him alone there to go through the pitifully few personal things that had been forwarded to them together with the usual letter from the Secretary of War regretting to inform them — the letter had said *killed on active service*, and Green felt guilty with the knowledge of how Rafferty had actually died, knowing no useful purpose would be served by telling them. The old man was no fool, though. He didn't fall for the story that Green had told about having to check Rafferty's personal effects for anything that might have pertained to his OSS work and could therefore be of potential value to an enemy of the United States. They didn't send an army major to do things like that. Green had fended the questions off as best he could. To tell the truth, he didn't know all the answers, anyway.

Three days ago he had been liaising with the British SOE office in Rockefeller Center, filling them in on details of his own missions behind German lines in 1944 and '45, and especially on his part in the smuggling out of Gisevius after *Valkyrie*, the July bomb plot which had just failed to kill Hitler. Without warning he had been told to report immediately to a Rear Admiral Sidney Souers at the Department of Justice in Washington, and within an hour of his arrival, Souers had taken him to see General George Marshall, Chief of Staff and principal adviser to the President.

He had followed Souers into Blair House with considerable trepidation, for what Souers had told him so far meant that he had that most detested of jobs, the prosecution of a case against a brother officer — in fact Rafferty would have been his nominal superior had he been working out of Washington instead of the Herrenstrasse in Bern.

A uniformed marine had led the way, opening door after door ahead of them until he finally stepped aside at a pair of floor-to-ceiling double doors, and they went into a room dominated by a huge table at the end of which, alone, sat Marshall.

'You've been fully briefed as to your task, Major?' Marshall rasped.

'Yes, sir,' Green replied.

'Sidney here thinks you're the man for the job. Looked at your record, got to agree.' He looked up as though daring Green to argue, his head tilted slightly back, mouth a fraction open. Green said nothing.

'Hm,' Marshall said. 'Well. You are to set up a headquarters at the Department of Justice. Ample funds will be placed at your disposal: all you'll need and more. A direct line between your office and mine will be set up. If you need anything moved that you can't move yourself, wherever you are, you are to telephone me and say, 'Jimmy wants to talk to George.' Got it?'

'Yes, sir.'

'I don't expect you need to be told that your investigation is to be kept completely secret. You will be given top security clearance wherever and whenever you need it. Every government department is being told to place its facilities at your disposal upon request. Get whatever staff you need together, do whatever you have to do. But find out everything there is to know about Rafferty. If he was passing information to the Russians I want every person he ever met talked to, every memo he ever wrote checked, every single stone turned over until we have all the answers. And I want them fast. Well — can you do it?'

'I can try, sir,' Green said.

'Do better than that,' Marshall said standing up to indicate that the interview was at an end. He shook hands with Green and turned to Souers. 'You'll keep me posted, Sidney?'

'We will, sir,' Souers said. 'Both of us.'

It had seemed logical to start at the beginning, and the beginning was Rafferty's home, his parents, his early life. The personnel dossiers had given the basic facts, but Green was looking for nuances, hints, the *feel* of the man. Unspectacular childhood — grade school, high school, college — the UCLA pennant, faded with the years, was still tacked to the wall — commissioned in 1941 (he grinned, remembering what they had called it in those days: a cellophane commission — you could see through them, but they kept the draft off), OSS training school in

Oshawa and later in Maryland, working his way up in Washington to the rank he had held when he had gone to Europe and his unexplained, inexplicable rendezvous with death.

Before he had left Washington, Green had put in hand a series of inquiries in New York, sent long and detailed cables to Toronto and to Naples, Italy. Hopefully, there'd be some sort of replies to them when he got back. He sat down on the bed in the little room, the heat of the day lingering still, looking at Rafferty's things. Many books: but nothing anywhere on politics, not even a general history. Hemingway, Wolfe, Fitzgerald, some popular novels, biographies of Washington, Pitt the Younger, piles of National Geographics — nothing to hint of any preoccupation with a world outside America. Records: Glen Miller, Tommy Dorsey, Sinatra, some Rodgers and Hart songs by Lee Wiley; Tchaikowsky and Rachmaninoff on twelve-inch seventy-eights. Old clothes, with nothing in the pockets but bus tickets, cinema ticket stubs, shreds of cigarette tobacco.

He opened the velvet-lined jewel box into which Martha Rafferty had put the few things sent back to her by the government. A wristwatch, a pocket knife, a cigarette case. He opened the pocket diary and his pulse quickened. Rafferty had been a diarist? He frowned. There were many blank pages. He got out his own notebook, looking for the dates he needed, turning the pages of the little leather-bound diary to May. In the space for 22 May Rafferty had written: *R called*! ! ! Green checked his own figures. The following day Rafferty had flown to Toronto. There was nothing entered for that day. The next entry was for 29 May. *See L*. L?' Rafferty had flown to New York that day. Who was L., who was R? Contacts? It was highly unusual for a spy to have more than one contact. For the 30th, Rafferty had made another cryptic entry. *Call J NY*. JNY? J. in NY? He turned the pages rapidly. Rafferty had scribbled — no, wait, it wasn't Rafferty's hand, someone else's — someone had scribbled a name and a telephone number on the page for 5 June. Hunter? Hirton?

No, Hinton. *Hinton ALB 884.3742*. A telephone number? What was ALB? Then more empty pages. Nothing until 12 June, and this the most cryptic of all. *S.* it read. *'HB EG H69-70 W150-60. Gitanes.'* The last entry was for 21 June, the day before Rafferty had been killed, and this one Green understood. *Galeriestrasse 33*, it said. The address of the apartment in which he had been killed.

He looked at the notes he had copied. Went through the rest of the diary. Except for Sunday, 6 May, there was nothing. There, just a telephone number? Green wrote it down. *J 725.5188*. Who had Rafferty called on VE Day? Was this the same J. of 30 May, J. in NY? Someone called — let's say — John, in New York, whose telephone number was 725.5188?

He lit a cigarette, watching the sun slide down towards the Pacific, the sky brazen with late summer heat. Cars swished by on Ninth Street outside. He looked at the notes on his lap.

6 May. J. 725.5188.
22 May. R. called!!!

29 May. See L.
30 May. Call J NY.
5 June. Hinton. ALB 884.3742.
12 June. S. HB EG H69–70
W150–60 Gitanes.
21 June. Galeriestrasse 33.

He got up. There was nothing else he could do here. Whatever secrets Michael Rafferty had had, and it looked from the diary entries that he had had some, he would not find the answers in this creaking old house. It was obvious that Rafferty had told his parents nothing about his life in Washington, nothing about his friends. They had received birthday cards, cards on their wedding anniversary, at Thanksgiving, gifts now and then, postcards if he was on vacation (Cape Cod, every time) but little else. He asked them if they knew any of Rafferty's friends, anyone with the initials L., or R., or J., anyone called Hinton. No. They hadn't known Michael's friends back east. He thanked them and left, promising to call them if he ever came back to Los Angeles. As he came out into the street he saw a cab unloading outside the Cromwell Hotel a couple of blocks away, and sprinted up the street. Ten minutes later he was at FBI headquarters downtown, and another ten minutes after that he knew that Ralph Hinton, of 1847 Twelfth Street, Albuquerque, New Mexico, had a son called Harwood who was a Lieutenant in the United States Navy, and that yes, Harwood had visited Naples in the summer. He pulled all the rank he could and got a seat on the Clipper to New York that night. A signal was on its way already to DNI in Washington, requesting that Hinton be located immediately and stand ready for interrogation. His phone call to the FBI had taken slightly longer. It wasn't much as a total. But it was a start.

18

18 September 1945

TELEX3875#BB445 WASHINGTON DC
9.18.1945
MOST URGENT TO MAJOR JAMES GREEN
1518 ROCKEFELLER CENTER NYC

YOUR EYES ONLY

PURSUANT YOUR INSTRUCTIONS THROUGH
COS WASHINGTON PRIORITY INVESTI-
GATIONS PUT IN HAND AS FOLLOWS

1) NEW YORK TELEPHONE 725.5188 REG-
ISTERED TO MISS JEANETTE DAVIDSON
APARTMENT 5B 226 WEST 48 STREET
NYC STOP DOSSIER ON DAVIDSON
FOLLOWING STOP SURVEILLANCE OF
APARTMENT AND TELEPHONE SET UP
AS OF FIVE AYEM THIS DAY STOP
2) ARMY MOTOR POOL NEW YORK HAS NO

RECORD ANY COLONEL RAFFERTY USING VEHICLE 29 MAY BUT MAN OF RAFFERTY'S DESCRIPTION USING NAME MAJOR JAMES LAWRENCE DRIVEN THAT DAY GREAT MEADOWS PENITENTIARY ALBANY WHERE HELD INCAMERA CONVERSATION WITH SALVATORE LUCIANIA ALIAS LUCKY LUCIANO AND LUCIANO LAWYER MOSES POLAKOFF STOP. ARMY RECORDS SHOW NO MAJOR JAMES LAWRENCE ATTACHED TO OSS STOP ALL OTHERS THAT RANK THAT NAME ACCOUNTED FOR STOP

3) MOVEMENTS RAFFERTY TORONTO STILL BEING CHECKED BUT NO DEFINITE WORD RECEIVED YET STOP

4) LIEUTENANT HARWOOD HINTON ARRIVING NAPLES AIR 20 SEPTEMBER STOP PLEASE ADVISE WHETHER YOU WISH FLOWN AMERICA OR AGENT TO INTERVIEW LOCALLY STOP

5) YOUR PUZZLE AN EASY ONE STOP SHORTENED DESCRIPTION OF SOMEONE WITH INITIAL S STOP HAIR BROWN EYES GREEN OR GREY HEIGHT FIVE NINE OR TEN WEIGHT ONE FIFTY OR ONE SIXTY SMOKES GITANES FRENCH

CIGARETTE BRAND STOP

NEXT TIME GIVE US SOMETHING DIFFI-
CULT STOP GOOD LUCK STOP HOOVER
+++ WNBBB3876#BBZ4459181945

19

Great Meadows, Albany
19 September 1945

James Green sat in the leather swivel-chair in the Warden's office at Great Meadows Penitentiary. In a few minutes they would be bringing Luciano in. His lawyer, Polakoff, was in the anteroom waiting. Green looked at his hands: they were trembling slightly with anticipation. What happened next could crack this business wide open. He leaned back in the chair and stretched, cracking his muscles. His whole body felt grainy, soiled, over-used, and the snatches of sleep he had managed in the car on the way up here had only made him aware of his need for more.

He'd done some homework on the man he was about to meet — Luciano had several filing cabinets all to himself at FBI headquarters in New York. It was an astonishing career, spanning as it did two generations of Mafia intrigue and murder, from the tiny village of Lercara Friddi in Sicily where Salvatore Lucania had been born in 1897 to the top of an organisation which by the mid-1930s was grossing more than $10,000,000 a year from prostitution alone. At fifteen, a petty thief; six months in jail for being in possession of heroin; leading light in New York's Five Points gang; by 1920, chief of staff to Giuseppe Masseria — until that *capo mafioso* had died beneath a hail of bullets in a Coney Island seafood restaurant, while Luciano, in the men's room, heard not a thing. By 1935 Luciano was running his own 'family' and had a suite in the Waldorf Astoria from which he masterminded most of the New York rackets: the waterfront, the garment industry, trucking, prostitution, under the name of 'Charles Ross.' But in that year a tough young special prosecutor named Tom Dewey had gone out after 'Mr Lucky' and nailed his hide to the barn door. Tried and found guilty on sixty-two counts of compelling women into prostitution (white slavery, the headlines of the day had called it) Luciano was sent down for a term of thirty to fifty, which the judge had probably fondly imagined meant life.

He'd been sent to Dannemora — 'Siberia', the cons called it — but within a year or two, he'd been running the place, a Don in prison to whom the other convicts came for help, for settlement of disputes, for punishment.

Green had read, too, the top secret files on the arrangements made with Luciano when Sicily had been invaded, and the files kept by a Lieutenant Commander Haffenden of the US Naval Reserve, who'd been co-ordinator of the arrangement which brought about Mafia intervention on the New York waterfront. Maybe Doctor Johnson had it right, at that, he thought; although, one day, someone might be very sorry for having forked over control of the heroin traffic to get laissez-passer through Sicily. He'd heard Luciano lived like a king up here at Albany. Great Meadows was no Siberia.

Give him a few more years, he'd probably be selling the guard girls, Green thought. He pushed a button on the desk and a few moments later a guard brought Luciano in. He was dressed in a short-sleeved open-weave shirt, dark-blue trousers, black loafers with tassels on them. He looked dark and Continental with a capital C, like the dancing instructors you sometimes still saw up on the west side. Gigolo was not a word Green used often, but that was what Luciano looked like. The door behind him opened, and Moses Polakoff came in. He looked at the guard, who nodded and went out. The Warden introduced them all and then looked at Green inquiringly.

'Stay,' Green told him. 'I want this on the record.'

He saw the glance Luciano exchanged with his lawyer, and was glad to see it had a slight touch of consternation in it.

'Mr Polakoff already explained to me why you was coming up here, Major,' Luciano said. He had a curious grating quality in his voice.

'What can I do for you?'

'On 29 May last you had a visit from a Major James Lawrence of the Office of Strategic Services,' Green began.

'I did?'

'You did, and I want to know what you talked about,' Green persisted.

Luciano turned to the lawyer. 'Do I have to answer?' Polakoff shook his head. Luciano grinned and turned back to face Green, spreading his hands.

'See Major? My hands are tied. I don't remember nothin'.'

Green looked at the mobster levelly.

'Mr Luciano,' he said. 'I want to know exactly what it was you talked about, and I want to know it now. I don't want to threaten you — '

'You?' Luciano sneered. 'You, threaten me?'

'But I want you to understand that unless you co-operate with me I will move heaven and earth to ensure that you stay here or go back to Dannemora until hell freezes over, and I want you further to understand that I have the power to do just that.'

'Moses,' Luciano said. 'Can he do this to me?'

Polakoff looked at Green, lighting a cigarette and squinting through the smoke.

'I don't know,' he said slowly. 'Can you, Major?'

'You'd better believe it.'

'Major Green is here on presidential authority,' the Warden said pompously. 'I think you'd be well advised — '

'You're bluffing,' Luciano said, ignoring the prison official.

'Okay,' Green said. 'We'll do it the hard way.'

He picked up the telephone and dialled a ten-figure number. There was a pause and then he heard the remembered voice at the other end.

'Jimmy wants to talk to George,' he said. He told General Marshall where he was and who he was talking to.

'I saw the file,' Marshall said. 'Put Polakoff on the line.'

Polakoff took the phone and listened. They saw his eyes widen, and then a flush of colour come into his cheeks. For the first time, a hint of respect came into the lawyer's expressionless face as he nodded, saying nothing, listening to the man in Washington.

'He wants to talk to you again,' he said to Green, holding out the telephone. As Green took the phone, Polakoff touched Luciano's arm and they went to the far side of the room, the lawyer whispering urgently into Luciano's ear.

'I told that sonofabitch who I am, who you are, and what he has got to do,' the Chief of Staff said. There was a chuckle in his voice as he asked, 'Did I scare the bejeezus out of him?'

'I think you did, sir,' Green replied.

'Good, good. Take whatever action you see fit, Major. If you want to send that heroin-peddling whoremonger to Devil's Island, damme if I don't try to fix it with the French. And you can tell him from me that if he thinks he's got any deal with the United States government he's labouring under the worst misapprehension since Napoleon at Waterloo. Do what you have to do, Major. And that includes shooting the bastard if you want to.'

'Thank you, General.'

'Keep me posted.'

The line went dead and Green put the receiver down, lifting his eyes to meet Luciano's. The mobster came across the room, pasting a smile on his face.

'Listen,' he said. 'You shoulda told us who you was. I mean, Christ, if you'd of said . . . '

'I'm told,' Green said levelly, 'that I can ship your ass off somewhere that'll make Dannemora look like Central Park if I want to. Frankly, I'd as soon do that as talk any more.'

Luciano looked at Polakoff again, but this time the lawyer made no signal.

'Now, Major,' Luciano said. 'Let's counsel on this, okay? We can make a deal, can't we?'

'No deal,' Green said. 'Talk.'

Again that look towards Polakoff. This time the lawyer nodded. Luciano sighed, spreading his hands again as if to say, 'what did I do?'

'Okay, okay,' he said. 'Here's what happened.'

★   ★   ★

Exactly six hours later, at 2100 hours New York time, Major James Green sat looking out of the porthole of a Boeing Super-fortress as its thundering engines lifted the huge machine clear of the runway at La Guardia and up across the flat dark waters of Long Island Sound. See Naples and die, he thought, remembering Rafferty.

20

Frankfurt
23 September 1945

'Have you seen these?'

'I've seen 'em.'

Colonel Donald Rogers tossed the American newspapers on Walt Gilchriese's desk with an exclamation of disgust.

''American General says Nazis are just like Republicans and Democrats'' he quoted. 'Campion's finally gone around the bend.'

'You'll find out soon enough,' Rogers replied. 'The Old Man's hotter than a two-dollar pistol. And you know what those tantrums of his are like.'

'What's on the agenda?'

'Staff meeting this pm at 1500 hours. He'll tell us then he's had a call from the White House. And that he's going to bust Campion.'

'Completely?'

'The works. He's going to take it all away from him. The Military Governorship, the Ninth Army, everything.'

'And where does that leave us?'

'Up shit creek,' Rogers said flatly. 'Without a paddle.'

There had been no way, of course, for anyone to plan for such a contingency. Campion had already been in hot water over a German he'd taken on for his staff at Bad Tölz, who turned out to have an SS dossier, and had gotten another reprimand from SHAEF for questioning their decision to get rid of a group of Bavarian industrialists who had had Nazi associations. Eisenhower had given him a mild warning in late August, and then a strongly-worded reprimand in a letter dated 12 September, in which Campion had been told in no uncertain fashion to stop playing up to the Germans by molly-coddling ex-Nazis. But on the 22nd, the ban on quoting general officers had been lifted, and Campion had called a press conference at his HQ. The press boys had been aware of the pressure that Campion was under from the top, and they had shafted him good.

Campion had said that the Military Government would get better results if it employed more former members of the Nazi party as administrators and skilled workers. They all knew what he meant, of course: it was the ex-Nazis who knew what had happened during the war, where the documents were, what had happened to court records, civil government files. But one of the correspondents had seen his chance and laid a nice neat deadfall for Campion.

'After all, General,' he had said, innocently. 'I suppose you could say that most Nazis joined their party the way Americans join the Democratic or Republican parties?'

'Exactly,' Campion had agreed, and the reporters had had their headline.

'Well,' Gilchriese said, heavily. 'So we cancel the Oshawa Project. No sweat.'

'Wrong,' Rogers said. 'We can't cancel it.'

'*What*?'

'Keep your voice down, damn you!' Rogers snapped. 'Come on, let's take a walk.'

Frowning, Gilchriese got up and followed Rogers out into the corridor. They took the elevator to street level and went out, returning the salute of the MPs at the door, walking close together. Turning the corner of the huge Farben headquarters they walked down the side into the shadows and sat on the low wall surrounding the car park.

'Now,' Gilchriese said. 'Explain.'

'I didn't tell you before,' Rogers said. 'I had Rafferty taken out.'

'You did what?'

'Will you quit saying *whaaaat* like that?' Rogers said testily, his voice rising a fraction. 'It was the right move at the time. He was the only link with us, with the Trust, everything. I couldn't take any chances. You know we talked about it.'

'I know we talked about it, Don. I just don't like it when you take action to terminate someone and don't pass it on. Jesus, what kind of stupid is that?'

'I know,' Rogers said. 'I'm sorry, Walt. It looked airtight.'

'I don't like the sound of that past tense,' Gilchriese said. 'What else are you

238

going to come up with?'

'It's gone to the top,' Rogers said. 'I got word from Taylor in Washington. They've cleared the decks — a full-scale investigation into Rafferty's movements, everything.'

'Jesus.' A pause, then. 'They can't get to us that way, can they?'

'No. No, I'm sure they can't.'

'Shelley?'

'Knows nothing about us.'

'But.'

'But — I don't think we want to take any chances. If Shelley is taken, it might be embarrassing but nothing more. I just don't like uncertainties. Especially when the project has been rendered pointless.'

'So?'

'We can ask our friends in Marseilles for help in trying to find him.'

'What for? If he can't point to us, what for? Why not just let him make the hit and disappear?'

'Two things. First, the investigation into Rafferty. We can't be sure he hasn't left something, some clue, that might point to us. It's not likely, but it's possible. Second, the man I used to take Rafferty out. He's gone missing. There's a chance the Russians may have picked him up. Oh, it's all right . . . ' he held up a hand to stem Gilchriese's imminent outburst. 'But it's another unexpected factor.'

'You want to get to Shelley?'

'We've got to, I think.'

'All right. I agree that. Now how do we go about it?'

'We wire ourselves in to the investigation. They've got a young OSS Major called Green handling it. I'll arrange to be kept informed of everything he finds out. It'll take a little more of the Fund. But it'll be money well spent. The minute he looks as if he's getting close, we can move.'

'If this Shelley is a pro, he won't be easy to take,' Gilchriese mused.

'Nobody's that good,' Rogers told him.

21

James Green knew what Jeanette Davidson looked like, long before she answered the door. He knew about her schooling, her hobbies, her illnesses, her dental repairs, her employers past and present, her friends, her parents; he had copies of her driving licence, her social security documentation, her PhD thesis on 'The American Musical — 1920 — 1940' for the Theatre and Arts Division of Columbia University, and an array of photographs taken of her by the FBI agents who had watched her continuously for the last six days. He knew that she was twenty-eight and that her hair was blonde, that she was five feet seven inches tall and had green eyes. But he was still unprepared for the fact that the blonde hair was long, and soft, and corn yellow, or for the dimples in the right cheek as she smiled and looked up at him.

'Miss Davidson?' he said. 'James Green. I called you earlier.'

'Oh, yes, Major,' she said. 'Come on in.'

She led the way into the living room, which was erratically furnished with odd pieces of furniture, a deep moquette-covered sofa facing a fireplace, two differently styled armchairs, one red, one black leather. A table in one corner served as a sort of bar. There were empty Coke bottles standing on it beside a stainless steel ice-bucket.

She turned to face him, touching her hair self-consciously.

'Sorry I'm got up to look like Tillie the Toiler,' she apologised, waving a slim-fingered hand at her smock and slacks. 'I was just cleaning the place up a little. We had some friends call by last night.'

'We?'

'My room-mate and I,' she explained. 'Jane's in publishing, too. She works in the publicity department at Scribner's.'

There'd been a dossier on Jane Perrin,

242

too. He hadn't paid much attention to it. Jeanette Davidson, Michael Rafferty's friend, was the one he wanted to meet.

Right up to this moment, he had wondered what, if anything, the girl was going to be able to tell him, or whether she had any of the missing pieces of the puzzle which was emerging. It was getting so every time he solved one part of the problem, the solution, itself became another problem. He knew Rafferty had used the name Lawrence for his meetings with Luciano and Esposito — but not why. Esposito had been unhelpful to the point of refusing even to discuss Rafferty/Lawrence or Shelley until he had spoken with New York. That had taken some doing, but it had been done, and Esposito explained the contact procedure: a *poste restante* number in Zürich which proved, sure enough, to have been rented by someone named Shelley. But the address given was a false one and that became another dead end. Green had talked to the young sailor, Hinton, hoping he might have something to add, but it was immediately apparent that his contact with Rafferty had been purely casual — he didn't even recall writing his phone number in Rafferty's diary until Green showed him the photocopy.

There were just too damned many 'whys'. Why Rafferty, of all people, had suddenly decided to take out an American general. Why he had hired a paid assassin. Why he had a bank account in San Francisco with more than $30,000 in it. Why he had gone to Oshawa, and who he had met there. Every single name and number in the diary had been checked out except the mysterious 'R' who had called, and Jeanette Davidson herself, who, according to the FBI agents keeping her under surveillance, was leading a totally normal, innocuous life. She spoke, interrupting his soliloquy of frustration.

'You said you wanted to talk about Mike,' she said.

'That's right,' he said. 'Was he a close friend?'

'Was?' she said, abruptly.

'I'm sorry,' he stammered. 'Didn't you . . . didn't you know?'

'He's . . . dead?' she said. 'Oh.' Then,

'Oh', again, sitting down on the sofa, her face stiff. Green cursed his own stupidity. It happened sometimes: you were so used to the idea, it never occurred to you that other people didn't know. She wouldn't have been listed as next of kin. Rafferty's parents hadn't even known she existed.

'I'm sorry,' he said.

'How . . . how did it happen?'

Her eyes were brimming with tears, but she wouldn't cry, he could see her fighting against it. One big teardrop rolled down her cheek and she sniffed, swallowing, lifting her chin slightly.

'He was killed in Munich,' he said gently. 'Nearly three months ago.'

'Oh,' she said, again. He could almost see the next question forming in her mind, and he anticipated it.

'It was a road accident,' he said, quickly.

She nodded, wordlessly.

'I'm sorry to have to do this, Miss Davidson,' he said. 'But I have to ask you some questions.'

'I understand,' she said. 'Were you . . . did you know Mike?'

'No, we never met. Although we were in the same branch of the service.'

'You're in intelligence?'

'Yes,' he said, thinking *how much did Rafferty tell her?* 'Did he talk to you much about his work?'

'Oh, no,' she said. 'He'd never discuss it. He used to make jokes about it, you know top secret, Jenny, by order of the President. Stuff like that.'

'Were you close friends?'

She wrinkled her nose, trying to say it exactly right.

'Not close-close,' she answered. 'But I liked him a lot, and we had good times. He used to come to visit me whenever he was in New York.' She said it the New York way. N'Yawk.

'How long had you known him?'

'Oh, a year, something like that. We met through friends. At Luchow's, you know, the — '

'I know the place.'

'He was in New York for a few days. Something to do with his work. We went out a couple of times. We both liked musicals. I did my PhD thesis on the

246

American musical.'

'Really?'

'Yes,' she said, and then unaccountably the tears came suddenly and she got up quickly from the sofa and went across to the window, looking out sightlessly at the blank face of the building opposite.

'When was the last time you saw him?'

'It must have been around the end of May,' she said. 'He called me from Washington to say he was coming to town the next day. He usually called first,' she explained, touching her lips with a slim forefinger. He wondered why he should be pleased that her finger-nails were unpainted. 'It was a surprise, actually, because he'd been here a couple of weeks earlier. He didn't usually get to New York that often.'

'Can you remember the dates? It's very important.'

She nodded, and went across the room to a bureau against the wall. From a drawer she pulled out a big desk diary, the kind you could buy in Ligget's for fifty cents. She riffled through the pages.

'6 May,' she said. 'I remember now, it

was VE Day. There were such crowds everywhere. We went to see *Oklahoma!* to sort of, you know, celebrate the end of the war in Europe.'

'And the next time?'

'29 May,' she said. 'He came about eight that night. Said he'd been upstate.'

'Did he stay here?'

Her chin came up and he saw a faint flush of colour stain her cheeks, but she answered without hesitation. 'Yes, he did. He went back to Washington the next evening.'

'Did he have a car?'

'No,' she said. She came back to the sofa and sat down again.

'All right, Major,' she said. 'I've answered all your questions. How about answering some of mine?'

'I'll try,' he said. 'But no promises.'

'What is all this about?'

'I beg your pardon?'

'Don't dissemble, Major,' she said, and for the first time he saw the hint of that dimple again. 'These questions about Michael . . . why are you asking them?'

'Sorry,' he said, 'I can't tell you that.'

'But you're investigating Michael's death?'

'Let me put it to you this way, Miss Davidson,' Green said. 'I'm trying to get a picture of Michael Rafferty's movements in the period preceding his death — where he went, who he saw, what he said, what state of mind he was in, a picture of him as he was just before he went to Europe. Did he tell you anything about his plans there?'

'No, he just said he had to go. I'd already learned not to ask him for details.'

'Did you hear from him at all when he was away?'

'Yes,' she said. 'He'd send a postcard, sometimes, or . . . '

Her eyes suddenly widened and her hand flew to her mouth.

'What is it?' Green said, getting to his feet.

'I just remembered,' she said softly. 'He sent me a letter after he left. He said to keep it until he got back. Not to open it: just keep it.

'Where is it?' snapped Green. 'Have you got it here?'

'Yes,' she said, 'yes, it's in the bedroom. Wait, I'll get it.'

He didn't wait, but followed her into the bedroom, catching the faint perfume of shampoo from her swinging hair. She reached up on tiptoe and slid a Lord & Taylor box down from the top of the wardrobe. He took it from her, snatching off the lid, spilling the contents on the bed. There were picture postcards, little kewpie dolls, souvenirs from Atlantic City, cocktail sticks with hotel names on them, letters.

'Which one is it?' he said.

She picked up a long 9 × 4 envelope, sealed at every join with brown sticky tape. On the front was written: *Jenny. Keep for me. Mike.*

'What did you think was in this?' Green said, ripping the envelope open. She half reached out a hand as if to prevent him from opening the envelope, then shrugged.

'I don't know,' she confessed. 'It was so unlike Michael, he was so serious. I thought it was his will or something.'

There were three sheets of ruled paper

covered with writing: Green recognised Rafferty's sloping hand immediately.

'What is it?' she asked. 'What does it say?'

'Where did he send this from?' Green said impatiently. 'Where's the envelope it came in?'

'Here,' the girl said. 'This one.'

The large yellow envelope had two pictorial Swiss 15c stamps in the right-hand corner. No return address. The postmark was 12 June 1945 and the letter had been mailed in Zürich, Switzerland. He read the whole thing through again, his heart racing. Now he had it all, and it was so unexpected, so impossible, that he could hardly believe the words he had just read.

Everything checked now, all the unrelated facts of Rafferty's movements that had been puzzling him, how he had got the travel documents that took him to Oshawa and New York and Naples and Zürich and Munich, all fitted together into a stunning, astonishing plot. He imagined Rafferty writing the letter in some hotel room, Shelley already lost by the OSS men from Bern he had used in a vain attempt to shadow the man, realising that the die was cast and perhaps simultaneously the potential danger he himself was in. To take out a kind of insurance, he had posted the letter to the girl in New York giving her all the details . . . the meeting in Oshawa, the alias he had used and why he had used it, the discussions with Luciano and Esposito, the deal with Shelley. And the other name, the one missing link that brought it all together.

'Quick, girl,' he said. 'Where's your telephone?'

22

'Come in, Judith,' Green said. 'Close the door.'

His secretary came into the office, a woman of about forty who had been seconded to him from the Justice Department. She was a plain, greying, pleasantly plump woman, quietly spoken, shy to the point of reticence. She was also tireless, efficient and indispensable to Green, and he liked her very much.

'Things are humming,' he remarked.

'They certainly are,' she said.

He glanced outside at the hubbub. His department had grown to formidable proportions, most of the extra people having been drafted in the last twenty-four hours, subsequent to his meeting in the Oval Room of the White House with the Joint Chiefs and the President.

Green had recognised only three of the men in the lofty, well-lit room. One was Souers, his immediate superior; the second was General Marshall; the third President Truman himself, immaculate in a double-breasted pearl-grey suit.

'Sit down, Major,' Truman had said, a friendly note in his rasping Missouri voice. 'Gentlemen, this is Major Green, who is attached to Rear Admiral Souers' National Intelligence Agency. It was he who unearthed the remarkable documents you have been reading.'

There was a murmur of greeting from the men around the highly polished table: enough brass, Green recalled thinking, to start World War Three all by themselves.

'We have concluded,' Truman said, his voice level and unemotional, 'that the matters contained in your briefing memorandum constitute one of the gravest — I hesitate to use the word astonishing, although, by God, I'm tempted to — gravest conspiracies which any American government has ever encountered. In fact, if it weren't for the letter Rafferty wrote, I'd still have trouble believing that the conclusions you have drawn had any foundation in sanity. But the Rafferty letter clinches it. I draw your attention once again, gentlemen, to the salient point outlined in Major Green's memorandum. Rafferty has been approached by a senior officer to hire an assassin to kill General Campion. The name of that senior officer is given but will not be put in writing anywhere, in any document, and memorandum, until Major Green indicates that he wishes it otherwise. In other words, the name of Colonel Donald Iselin Rogers is not to be mentioned in this context anywhere outside this room.'

He looked up, the sharp eyes narrowed behind the rimless glasses.

'Understood?' There was no reply, nor did he seem to expect one.

'Major Green will now continue with the investigation into the plot which he has so successfully penetrated. He will endeavour, correction, he *will* establish all of the facts, track down all or as many of the participants as it is possible to do.

'I'm one of the few presidents,' he said with a faint smile, 'who likes to avoid imperatives. But you must find these men, Major. You must find — and stop — this Shelley.'

'Yes, sir,' Green had said.

'You appreciate, I'm sure,' General Marshall put in softly, 'the delicacy of your assignment, how many reputations — not the least, if I may say so, Mister President, your own and that of the late President Roosevelt — rest upon your bringing it to a satisfactory conclusion.'

'You will spare no expense,' Truman said, 'no effort, and no person — least of all any of us here — in achieving results, Major. Clear so far?'

'Yes, sir.'

'Anything you need — staff, money, transportation, anything, all you'll have to do is ask for it and you'll get it. Clear?'

'Yes, sir,' Green had said again.

Truman's flinty face had softened a little, and he permitted himself another faint smile.

'There'll be one, ah, minor change in your arrangements, Major,' he said.

'The direct-line set-up with General Marshall's office will also be looped into the White House. You'll still use the same code. The difference will be that you may sometimes get me on the line. I sometimes have almost as much clout as George does.'

There had been dutiful laughter around the table. Nobody in that room had been in any doubt about Truman's clout since the first week of August when he had given the go-ahead to drop the atomic bomb on Hiroshima.

'Night or day,' Truman said. 'If you want action — call.'

'Yes, sir. Thank you.'

'Good,' Truman said. He got up and came around the table, shaking Green's hand warmly. 'Good luck, Godspeed, boy,' he said. 'You're going to need it.'

Damned right, Green reflected. He thought he'd been working hard so far but the flow of material coming now was astonishing.

'Okay,' he said harshly, shaking off the reverie. 'Let's go. First, a memo to Charlie Gross in Berne.'

He instructed Gross to set up immediately a three-man bodyguard for General

Campion. The bodyguard was to be with Campion twenty-four hours a day, seven days a week, wherever he went, whatever he did. He also asked Gross to send a list of the General's advance engagements, where known, and to watch particularly for any regular pattern of activities which could be homed in on by a potential assassin, defusing by altering it. He knew, and he knew Charlie knew, that there was no way in which a determined man with a high-powered rifle could be prevented from killing another who, by the nature of his occupation, frequently appeared in crowded public places. But aside from that, he knew Charlie would do a good job, get the best men. They had worked together in North Africa.

'Now, a list,' he told his secretary.

'In Britain: SIS, SOE, MI5, Scotland Yard.

'In Switzerland: Stadtpolizei, Kantonspolizie, Fremden-polizei Bern. In France: Sûreté Nationale and Deuxième Bureau (check whether they're fully operational yet, will you?).

'In Germany: SHAEF HQ: ask for a

full check of all Geheime Staatspolizei — that's Gestapo — records.

'Get the rest of them from the State Department, make a list of all the names and addresses of the top men in each. Send them the description we have of Shelley — the one the OSS people in Bern turned up — and get a special covering cable from the President to go with it.' He smiled. 'Got all that?'

She nodded, scribbling furiously.

'Next, a telex to the Secretary of State. I want the passport documents of every American male over twenty-one who fits Shelley's description checked — I know, dammit, I know — and particularly, and with utmost priority, all people having that name or those initials. A copy of that telex to all the people on your list for information and, if possible — although I doubt we'll get it — action. Right?'

'Right,' she said.

'To heads of state police forces — and every one of the 48,' he grinned, 'a memo asking specifically for details of any unsolved murder or suspicious accidental death where a description of someone like our man is on file. You might feed that one over to FBI, too, just in case they haven't already thought of it.'

'Roger,' she said.

'What?'

'Roger,' she said faintly, ducking her head.

'What the hell does that mean?'

'It's . . . it's what British pilots say to each other. In their fighters, I mean. I saw it in a Leslie Howard movie, *The First of* . . .

'Spare me,' he groaned, theatrically. He handed her three sheets of paper:

'Can you read that?'

'I think so,' she said.

'Transcribe it, and make five copies.'

'What is it?' she asked.

'Rafferty's last will and testament,' he grinned. 'That's the letter that broke the whole thing wide open, my love, so take good care of it. And don't let it or the copies out of your hands under any circumstances. Okay?'

She smiled and got up, her notebook tight against her chest. He was already buried in the papers on his desk, a frown of concentration twisting his young face into a furious grimace. She went back to her desk and sat down, reading through Rafferty's three-page letter with widening eyes. When she had finished, she laid it down gently, as if it might break, leaning back in her chair, her eyes empty. Then slowly, as if in a dream, she reached for the telephone.

'Homer' the voice at the other end said.

'Judith,' she replied. 'Two o'clock. Usual place.'

'Confirmed,' the voice said.

Then Judith Coplon typed a neat copy of the letter Rafferty had sent to Jeanette Davidson in New York. She made six carbons. Within three hours one of them was in the Russian Embassy and in another two transmitted in code to Moscow.

23

Moscow
28 September 1945

The Intelligence Department of the Red
Army, or RU, as it was known, was based
in an old baroque palace at 19 Znamensky. Its head was General Golikov, a
Colonel General of the Army who held
the title Director of Army Intelligence.
His assistant, Major General Fyodor
Kuznetzov, was his direct link with the
several major divisions (and their regional
activities) each headed by a colonel with
the title Organiser. Their Department was
known as 'the Centre' in Soviet intelligence parlance and in the parlance of
their allies and enemies.

These two, Golikov and Kuznetzov, sat
now in an echoing room on the ground
floor of the Centre. Golikov was a short,
rather fat man with a somewhat prehen-
sile chin and sharp blue eyes, who

affected full dress uniform and medals at all times. There were some who considered him to be a mountebank, but his abilities as Director of Army Intelligence were never questioned. Kuznetzov was tall, thin and stooping, for all the world like some university professor with short-sighted eyes swimming behind thick-lensed steel-rimmed glasses. He smelled like a stoat, and the third man at the table wrinkled his features in disgust. These Political Division people were necessary, he knew. One only wished that sometimes they would wash. He pulled a large silk handkerchief from his pocket and blew his nose gustily. The others watched him, waiting for him to speak, deferential in his presence: for this was Lavrenti Beria, head of the Soviet Secret Police, People's Commissar for Internal Affairs, answerable only to Stalin himself.

If Beria found the Political Division people distasteful, they found him totally disgusting. His sexual peculiarities were known to everyone in the capital, his perversions as dreadful to contemplate as they were impossible to mention.

'Is there nothing to drink in this mausoleum?' Beria demanded, breaking the timorous silence with his huge peasant voice.

'Of course, of course, Comrade,' Golikov said. He opened a cabinet and brought out a bottle of vodka and some glasses. Beria poured a half tumbler full and muttering *Vashe zdorovye!* swigged it down, the liquor dribbling from the corners of his mouth on to his chin. Golikov looked at his deputy and smiled faintly, lifting his own glass and sipping the drink.

'You drink like a woman, Comrade!' Beria shouted, laughing aloud and pouring another drink. 'Well, let's hear from you, man! Why are we here, eh, why are we here?'

'We have some intelligence which leads us to believe that we may be able to bring about a situation which will profoundly embarrass the American military in Europe,' Golikov said. 'Before proceeding, I wished to ensure that my suggestions would not in any way interfere with any plans the Comrade

Commissar' — Beria smiled fatly at the fulsome title — 'might be either considering or implementing.'

'Let's hear it, then,' Beria said, guzzling down another glass of the vodka.

'Let me start at the beginning,' Golikov said. 'It is rather a complicated matter.'

Beria grunted and looked ostentatiously at his watch.

'Don't take all night, that's all,' he said. 'I want to get some fresh air before I go to bed.'

Golikov's lip curled in disgust and fear. Everyone knew what Comrade Beria did before he went to bed. He drove around the streets and —

'Come on, man, we'll be here all night!' Beria growled.

'In July this year,' Golikov said, 'A man was stopped at a checkpoint in Berlin.'

'22 July,' Kuznetzov added.

'He was carrying, among other things, a Swiss passport, a pistol, and about eighteen hundred American dollars.'

'The point, the point, get to the point,' Beria snapped.

'He was questioned — fortunately one

of our people was nearby and sent for,' Kuznetzov said, with deadly precision. 'Before he died, he told us that he had been hired to assassinate an American intelligence officer in Munich, a Major Michael Rafferty. He said the man who hired him was an American whom he thought was an officer.'

'This was in Frankfurt,' Golikov added.

'Go on,' Beria said heavily. Good, Golikov thought, he's getting interested.

'In August, two things happened almost simultaneously,' Golikov said. Better get this over with. 'First, the British broke one of our ciphers — for a very short period only,' he added hastily, seeing Beria's frown deepen.

'We were well covered, but they did establish that we had been asking Station 15 . . . '

'Washington,' Kuznetzov interpreted.

' . . . about this Rafferty,' the Director continued. 'I'll come back to that in a moment. The second thing that happened was that one of our people tried to go across to the British in Istanbul.'

'Volkov,' Kuznetzov supplied helpfully.

'I know about him,' Beria growled.

'Yes, indeed, Comrade Commissar,' Kuznetzov said. 'It was your Department which brought the man back for correction.'

'I personally took charge of the interrogation of friend Volkov,' purred Beria, as if they had reminded him of something especially pleasant. 'How the swine squealed and bled. He took a very long time to die.'

Golikov looked at his deputy and shrugged very slightly.

'Thanks to . . . thanks to our contact in the Foreign Office, we were able to prevent an unfortunate leakage, although I do not think Konstantin Volkov was in a position to offer the British very much classified information, eh, Kuznetzov?'

'I think not, sir,' said Kuznetzov with a prim smile.

'So,' Beria said. He leaned forward and took the bottle of vodka by the neck, tipping it back and pouring it down his pulsing throat.

'Have you had confirmation of that from that drunken fool in London?' Beria asked, putting the empty bottle down with a bang on the polished table.

'The British intelligence people passed the snippets they had on to the Americans,' Golikov replied. 'They lay dormant because President Truman had just disbanded the Office of Strategic Services. Then early this month, the new security organisation . . . '

'The National Intelligence Authority,' Kuznetzov said.

' . . . began an investigation into Rafferty's death on the suspicion according to our contact in the Department of Justice, that he was a Russian spy.'

'And was he?' Beria asked.

'No, no, Comrade Commissar,' Golikov held up a hand to fend off such a silly idea.

'Where is all this leading?'

'It is not *leading* anywhere, Comrade Commissar,' Kuznetzov said. 'This much is purely background information.'

'Christ on the cross!' shouted Beria. 'I'll need something more to drink if I'm to sit here all night listening to this double-act. Golikov!'

The Colonel General reached into the cabinet and brought out another bottle. He sometimes wished there was some way he could claim for extra rations on the grounds that most of his own were drunk by the higher-ups who came constantly into his office and demanded something. He could hardly go into Commissar Beria's sanctum and bellow for drink. He'd be in Siberia before he could say *ochen horosho*. 'I would now like you to read a document which our contact in the Department of Justice has passed to us,' Golikov said. 'It is a letter written by the man Rafferty before he went to Europe from America.'

'Translated, of course,' Kuznetzov added.

'I can read English,' glared Beria. He slouched in his chair, his lips moving as he went through the neatly-typed page. He sat up, his eyes suddenly bright, searching.

'And what else have we?'

Golikov smiled. This was his moment.

'The complete dossier compiled by the officer in charge of the investigation in Washington.'

There was silence in the room for a long time as Beria pored over the file, his clumsy hands spread flat on the sides.

'And this information,' growled Beria. 'How reliable is it?'

'Absolutely,' Kuznetzov said.

'Yes, absolutely,' confirmed Golikov. 'The woman Coplon in the Department of Justice is totally reliable. And you yourself, Comrade Commissar, referred a few moments ago to the fact that the Englishman, Philby, prevented the defection of Volkov. So you may rely upon information he provides us with.'

'This man in Washington, then,' Beria persisted. 'Homer, Burgess, whatever you call him. Another Englishman. Can you trust him?'

'I doubt if anyone could,' Golikov said urbanely. 'But he is useful as a courier and well connected. That is all.'

'So,' Beria said. 'They plan to assassinate Campion — the best general they have. What motive, what reason is behind this plan?'

'We believe that he has become politically embarrassing to them.

'His remarks about ourselves in particular have been highly inflammatory. If you wish to see the file . . . ?'

'No,' Beria said, waving it aside. 'I'll take your word for it. What's your plan?'

'Simply,' Kuznetzov said, 'to capture this assassin before the Americans can do so. And to make public his confession that he was hired by an American officer to assassinate a general of the United States Army.'

'It would be a tremendously effective political blow, Comrade Commissar,' Golikov said softly, 'which could perhaps considerably influence public opinion on the question of — for example — Berlin.'

Beria nodded. 'Yes, I see that,' he said. 'The question I ask you is: do we take him before, or after, he has committed the assassination?'

'Without doubt afterwards,' Golikov said firmly.

'I agree,' said Kuznetzov.

'So do I,' said Beria, to their surprise. 'Very well. It is a good plan. Put it into operation immediately.'

'He will be difficult to find, this man

Shelley,' Kuznetzov said, hesitantly.

'But not impossible?'

'No,' Golikov said slowly. 'Not impossible, I think.'

'Good,' Beria said, getting to his feet like a bear in a pit going after a titbit thrown down to him.

'You will give this matter priority,' he said. It was not said as a question, nor yet an order. But Golikov and Kuznetzov both knew it was a command, for all that.

'Of course, Comrade Commissar,' Golikov said, urbanely.

'Keep me informed,' Beria said, starting for the door. He stopped, and came back, picking up the half-empty vodka bottle in a huge paw. 'Keep me informed,' he repeated, and went out through the huge oak doors. Golikov and Kuznetzov watched him go. Neither said anything, but they looked at each other and both nodded. Beria was a monster, the worst kind of human being. But his power was immeasurable, total, and neither of them had any intention of falling foul of it.

Golikov nodded and shuffled the papers in front of him into an orderly pile. He stood up and stretched.

'Get things started,' he told Kuznetzov. The Deputy Director picked up the telephone and spoke at length to the Communications Department in the dank basement below the old palace. Within a short while the 'musicians' were sending out messages on their 'music boxes' to every Soviet Embassy and Consulate in the world. The Red Army Intelligence Department had something between a quarter of a million and four hundred thousand agents and operatives throughout the world. Within twenty-four hours every one of them would be looking for Shelley. They had a little less than three months in which to find him.

24

Washington
29 September 1945

TELEX 4482#DJ616 WASHINGTON DC
0945 929, 1945 ENCODED BEFORE
SENDING MOST URGENT TO MAJOR
CHARLES GROSS
  IN CARE COMMAND HQ NINTH ARMY
YOUR EYES ONLY

★　★　★

WE HAVE A POSSIBLE YOUR AREA
STOP PETER SHELLEY LISTED AS
FREELANCE CORRESPONDENT BASED
MUNICH ADDRESS AGNESSTRASSE 66
FITS DESCRIPTION OUR MAN STOP
CHECK AND ADVISE IMMEDIATELY
STOP GREEN STOP ENDIT
448261609451011945 — 66 ENCODED
NN#CD3338 1030
HRS SENT±

* * *

TELEX 8679#9ABT BAD TOLZ 1830 929,
1945 ENCODED BEFORE SENDING MOST
URGENT TO MAJOR JAMES GREEN DEPT
JUSTICE WASH DC

* * *

YOUR EYES ONLY

* * *

SHELLEY KNOWN HERE STOP WORKS
FREELANCE LOCAL JOURNALS STOP
CONTRIBUTES TO HEUTE MAGAZINE
ALSO NEUE ZEITUNG BOTH MUNICH
STOP CAMPIONS COMMUNICATIONS
OFFICER HAS SHELLEY ON BRIEFING
LISTS FOR INVITATION ANY PRESS
CONFERENCES GIVEN ARMY HERE
STOP ADDRESS AGNESSTRASSE 66
CHECKS OUR RECORDS STOP WHAT
INSTRUCTIONS QUERY STOP GROSS
STOP ENDIT
   867991830101194566   ENCODED
FG#BT769 1902 HRS SENT±

TELEX 4486#DJ616 WASHINGTON DC 1330 929, 1945 ENCODED BEFORE SENDING MOST URGENT TO MAJOR CHARLES GROSS IN CARE COMMAND HQ NINTH ARMY

* * *

YOUR EYES ONLY

* * *

IMPERATIVE CHECK FASTEST SHELLEY PRESENT WHEREABOUTS ALSO ASSIGN-MENTS IF ANY LAST SIX MONTHS HEUTE AND NEUE ZEITUNG STOP ADVISE IMMEDIATELY STOP GREEN STOP ENDIT 448661612301011945 ENCODED NN#CD3338 1350 HRS SENT±

* * *

TELEX 8682#9ABT BAD TOLZ 2020 929, 1945 ENCODED BEFORE SENDING MOST

URGENT TO MAJOR JAMES GREEN DEPT
JUSTICE WASH DC

★ ★ ★

YOUR EYES ONLY

★ ★ ★

SORRY DELAY STOP NEEDED AUTHOR-
ITY OPEN HEUTE OFFICE DITTO NEUE
ZEITUNG
   HEREWITH LISTING ARTICLES CON-
TRIBUTED SHELLEY PAST SIX MONTHS
STOP DATELINE 18 JUNE SWITZERLAND
NEVER HAD A WAR BUT STILL FEELS THE
EFFECTS OF EVERYONE ELSES ABOUT
2000 WORDS SOME PICTURES STOP
DATELINE 25 JUNE SWITZERLAND,
HOLIDAY PARADISE IN SPITE OF RATION-
ING 2500 WORDS NO PIX STOP BOTH
HEUTE MAGAZINE STOP NEXT DATE-
LINE 23 JUNE MUNICH RISES FROM
RUBBLE BIRTH OF A NEW KIND OF
GERMAN CITY IN NEUE ZEITUNG
ABOUT 3000 WORDS NO PIX STOP
NOTHING THEN UNTIL DATELINE 3

SEPTEMBER MUNICH CELEBRATES VIC-
TORY IN JAPAN IN HEUTE MAGAZINE
ABOUT 2500 WORDS NO PIX STOP
DATELINE 23 SEPTEMBER AMERICAN
GENERAL DEFENDS NAZI REGIME JUST
LIKE REPUBLICANS AND DEMOCRATS
SAYS CAMPION IN NEUE ZEITUNG
ABOUT 1500 WORDS STOP EDITORS
BOTH JOURNALS SAY SHELLEY CON-
TRIBUTES STUFF ON A SPECULATIVE
BASIS AND PAID IF PUBLISHED $50 PER
1000 WORDS STOP RARELY SEE HIM
PERSONALLY STOP HIS REJECTED
STUFF NOT KEPT STOP WHAT THE HELL
IS ALL THIS STOP GROSS STOP ENDIT
8682920201011944518200025250023300
0325002315005010   ENCODED
FG#BT771 2100 HRS SENT±

* * *

TELEX 4489#DJ616 WASHINGTON 1614
929,1945 ENCODED BEFORE SENDING
  MOST URGENT
  TOP PRIORITY YOUR EYES ONLY

* * *

MAJOR CHARLES GROSS IN CARE COM-
MAND HQ NINTH ARMY

★   ★   ★

IMPERATIVE PLACE SHELLEY UNDER
IMMEDIATE SURVEILLANCE ESPECIALLY
IF ANY LIKELIHOOD HIS BEING PROXIM-
ITY CAMPION STOP APPREHEND ONLY
REPEAT ONLY IF OVERT ACTION IMMINENT
STOP ESSENTIAL WARN ALL PERSONNEL
SHELLEY PROBABLY ARMED AND DAN-
GEROUS STOP TAKE ABSOLUTELY NO
CHANCES OF SCARING HIM OFF STOP
FLYING MUNICH IMMEDIATELY STOP
MEET WITH TRANSPORT STOP GREEN
STOP ENDIT
    44891616141011945 ENCODED
NN#CD3338 1624 HRS SENT±

★   ★   ★

TELEX 8684#9ABT BAD TOLZ 2240
929,1945 ENCODED BEFORE SENDING
TOP PRIORITY SIGNAL YOUR EYES ONLY

★   ★   ★

MAJOR JAMES GREEN DEPT JUSTICE
WASH DC

★ ★ ★

SHELLEY NOT AT AGNESSTRASSE STOP
LEFT EARLIER TODAY BELIEVED ASSIGN-
MENT BUT EXACT DESTINATION
UNKNOWN STOP SORRY JIM BUT YOUR
INSTRUCTIONS TWO HOURS TOO LATE
STOP PLEASE ADVISE STOP GROSS STOP
ENDIT
  8864922401011945 ENCODED
FG#BT769 2255 SENT±

25

Munich
29 September 1945

'Darling,' Theresa von Rodeck said. 'Darling Elli.'

As she snuggled against him on the sofa, Colonel Elton Stewart leaned back against the soft cushions, his whole body completely, utterly relaxed. This was the way to spend a Saturday night, by God, he thought, especially after the kind of day he'd had. Indeed, it had seemed as if there was some sort of conspiracy to prevent him getting down to town at all — some jerk in Washington tying up the telex for hours on end, with that intelligence fellow, Gross, and Campion's G2 Cook hopping around like long-tailed cats in a room full of rocking chairs. He grinned. That was one of the old man's sayings back home in Macon, Georgia. He hadn't thought about the old man for a long time. He hadn't thought about home in a long time, come to that. He felt the supple hardness of Theresa against his chest, and the glow of her sated body brought back their last hour in the bedroom. Holy shit, she could do it, he thought. The last few weeks, tell the truth, he'd been thinking that maybe he ought to dump her delectable little ass right in the middle of the Prinzregentenstrasse, so tightlipped and nervous and bitchy had she become. All that jumping every time the phone rang, every time a car pulled up in the Lerchenfeldstrasse outside. If he objected, mildly, she sprang at him, all tongue and claw and poison; a bitch incarnate. Then tonight, just like it had been right at the beginning. There had been candles at the table, and she'd worn the nightdress he'd had one of his sergeants bring back from leave in Paris, the one with the cutaway panels and the lacy frills that exposed her breasts and buttocks, teasing him at first, her hands and mouth all over him, urging and then preventing, until they had come together in a mounting, furious tangle on the black sheets. Now, after they had dozed together on the bed and he had bathed, the warm glow in his belly from the lovemaking and the cognac in his hand, Stewart felt at peace with the world. Yes, sir, he thought again: this was the only way to spend Saturday night.

'Darling,' she whispered, her face against his chest. 'You're so good to your *Schätzi*.'

'Mmmmm,' he said, feeling a protective glow.

'You wouldn't let anything awful happen to me, would you, Elli?'

'Of course not,' he said, kissing the top of her head. Her hair smelled of shampoo and perfume. Nice, he thought, sighing contentedly.

'You're so good,' she sighed. 'You look after me so well.'

'Mmmm,' he said, sipping the cognac. 'I always will, *Liebchen*.'

'Even if I do something bad?' she asked, in a small voice.

He smiled. 'You?' he said, lifting her face with his left hand, surprised to see tears in her eyes. 'Why, what is it, honey?'

'Oh, Elli,' she said, starting to cry properly now, her shoulders shaking a little. 'I can't tell you.'

'Don't worry, *Schatz*,' he said. 'You can tell Elli.'

She shook her head, wordlessly, tears dropping onto her bare legs. She sniffed and got up, leaving him staring at her, frowning.

'Theresa,' he said.

'No, Elli, I'm sorry,' she said. 'It would mean . . . it would mean you wouldn't want to see me any more. It would mean . . .'

'Hey, now,' he said, gently, not worried yet. 'Come on, honey. You know I wouldn't treat you bad. Tell me what's bothering you?'

He got up and went over to the table, pouring her some cognac and refilling his own glass.

'Here,' he said. 'Drink this. Come and sit down. Come on.'

She let him lead her back to the sofa and then put the drink down, her arms going around his neck, holding him tight.

'Elli, Elli,' she said, 'I'm so frightened.

So very frightened. I don't want to lose you. Promise me I won't lose you.'

'I promise,' he said, taking her arms in his own hands, putting them down into her lap, looking into her tear-filled eyes. 'Look,' he said. 'I promise, whatever it is, we'll still be together. I love you, Theresa.'

Theresa von Rodeck raised her eyes, her lips tremulous, face filled with hope. 'You mean it?'

'Sure, honey,' Stewart said, thinking: *women*, wondering what petty tale of over-spending, of over-indulgence, she was going to tell him.

'I'm being blackmailed,' she said.

'What?'

'I'm being blackmailed. Because of you,' she repeated.

He sat there looking at her, feeling as if someone had just thrown iced water all over him. He felt a flutter of fear inside his stomach, mind racing over a thousand possibilities, options, eventualities, conclusions, not able for a moment to think clearly. Then his mind snapped together, logical once more.

'Tell me,' he said. 'Sit down here and

tell me everything.'

She told him the whole story: the story that she had worked out carefully only two evenings before with Reinhard, a story near enough to the truth to be convincing, but not so truthful that he would baulk and simply offload her. They weren't ready yet to say goodbye to the apartment and the food and the easy living, not yet. But they had to remove the threat posed by possible exposure of Theresa's past. And they had worked out a way to do it.

Theresa von Rodeck could tell the American was swallowing it. He listened carefully, but sympathetically, as she explained how, immediately after the end of the war, starving in the streets, she had agreed to pose for some photographs. She hadn't known then, of course, what was to happen. But they had given her so much to drink she hadn't known what she was doing, and they had taken photographs of her doing bad things.

'You mean pornographic pictures?' he said.

'Yes, Elli,' she said contritely.

'And now someone is asking for money for them, is that it?'

'Not money, darling,' she said.

The man had come to see her and told her he wanted information. About the movements of certain people at Bad Tölz. General Campion especially. She had been forced to agree, he saw that, didn't he?

'I get it now,' he said. His voice had gone dull, flat. She knew this was the hardest part.

'Oh, Elli, darling,' she said, throwing herself into his arms, kissing his neck, his face, using all of herself to convince him. 'I hated it, I hated it, every moment of it. But I was afraid. He said he would send the photographs to your Commanding Officer, and I was frightened in case he hurt you, my darling.'

'The bastard,' she heard him growl, and a feline smile touched her mouth.

'Elli, Elli,' she murmured. 'What can I do, I can't go on any longer living this lie when I love you so much, so much, so much my darling . . . '

'Yes,' he said, absently. He kissed her,

then kissed her mouth hard, his lips hot, worrying at her, pushing her back against the cushions, demanding her body again. He started to pull off the robe he was wearing, his hands pulling at her panties, but she eeled out of his hands, leaving him panting heavily, looking up surprised.

'Elli, darling,' she said. 'I want to as well, but that's what I was trying to tell you. Every Saturday, ten thirty on the dot, he telephones for the information. If I don't answer, he'll just send the photographs to Bad Tölz. He swore he would, that's why I'm so frightened.'

'You . . . you're right,' Stewart said. He got up and tied the robe around himself. Come on, Stewart, he told himself, you're not thinking. If he's got a hold on the girl, he's probably also well aware of the fact that she's being kept by Colonel Elton F. Stewart of the 9th Army, and if he sends that information to GHQ, Campion is going to blow so many fuses it will look like the Fourth of July up there. His mind raced: assessing, discarding possibilities again. Before he could make any real decision, the phone rang. He looked at his watch. 10.30. He nodded to Theresa, who picked up the phone. He padded across beside her, his ear to the receiver.

'Von Rodeck,' she said.

'It's me,' said the voice at the other end.

'I know,' she said.

'What have you got for me this week?' the voice asked.

She looked at him with wide eyes. *Stall him*, he mouthed, taking the pad and pencil beside the phone and scribbling furiously.

'Just a moment,' she said. 'I wrote it down.'

Campion's movements? Stewart had written. Yes, she nodded urgently.

He nodded and wrote again, *Anything else?* No, she signalled.

'A moment more, please,' she said, gesturing *hurry, hurry*.

'I never knew generals led such dull lives,' she said.

'Just information, Theresa,' the voice said. 'I can do without the social niceties.'

'It's not worth telling,' she said angrily, watching Stewart scribbling, her eyes anguished with suspense. 'I've been telling you all this time, it's always the same: he goes to a dinner, he opens a new PX. He is visiting field headquarters somewhere or other. He is having dinner with some officers in town. He's staying on the base. It's stupid. Why do you want to know such stupid things?'

'I'm writing a biography,' was the imperturbable reply. 'Now please stop wasting my time, Theresa,' *Oh God, Klaus, please be patient . . . I am trying so hard, so . . .*

'Very well,' she said. 'Monday through Wednesday on the base. Thursday Frankfurt at SHAEF HQ for a personal meeting with Eisenhower . . . '

'I was wondering how long it would be,' she heard him murmur. 'Go on, go on.'

'After the meeting to Speyer — staying until the following Sunday?'

She put her hand over the mouthpiece and turned to Stewart.

'He wants to know why he's going to Speyer, where it is.'

'Tell him he's going hunting, it's near Mannheim.'

290

She repeated the information into the telephone.

'You sure of this?'

'Yes, I'm sure,' she said. 'That's what the American told me.'

She grimaced apologetically at Stewart, who nodded, making a signal that she should hang up.

'You've done well, little Theresa,' she was told.

'Yes, yes,' she said, 'is that all?'

'That's all. Same time next week, little one.'

'Damn you!' she ground out, forgetting for the moment that Stewart was there. 'When is this going to end?'

'Very soon, *Liebchen*,' the voice said, and then the line went dead. She slammed the phone down on the hook, breasts rising and falling with the anger inside her. She snatched the cigarette Stewart offered her, getting control as she puffed on it furiously.

'You see?' she said, shrilly. 'You see why I have been so nervous, so jumpy, now? That . . . that . . . '

Stewart put his arm around her and led

her across to the sofa.

'It's all right, honey,' he said. 'It's all right. Let Elli take care of it.' He kissed her ear, soothing her, until she turned to him and smiled, honey-sweet and softening.

'Oh, Elli, I'm glad you were here,' she said. 'I'm glad I told you. I've been so worried, so afraid.'

'It's going to be all right,' he said. 'All we have to do is wait until next week. I can work something out. But you've got to tell me everything, Theresa, everything.'

'Yes,' she said. 'Yes, I will, *Liebchen*.'

'Good,' he said. 'Now, has he ever been here?'

She hesitated for a moment; he felt her stiffen slightly. Then she relaxed again in his arms.

'Yes,' she said. 'Once.'

'Good,' he replied. 'Then he might come again. If he had reason to?'

'I suppose so. Why?'

'Don't you worry about that,' he told her. 'If we can get him to come here, I can get a couple of friends of mine, MPs, to pick him up. And take him somewhere nice and quiet. Talk to him, persuade him to see the error of his ways.' He grinned wickedly.

She got up from the sofa, her eyes bright again, dancing with the clean pleasure of a child who has been told she won't be punished. She kissed him lightly on the lips, going across the room to pour more cognac into their glasses.

'Oh, Elli,' she said happily, coming back to sit beside him. 'I knew you'd understand, I knew you'd help me.'

He leaned back as she nuzzled his throat, her hands moving beneath the robe. 'Let us forget him,' she murmured. 'Just for the rest of tonight, let us forget Mr Shelley and his . . . '

He was on his feet in an instant, his eyes narrowed and frightened, face chalk white and drawn.

'What did you say?' he hissed, his eyes blazing at her.

'Elli, darling, what is it?' she mewled.

'The name, damn you!' he shouted. 'The name!'

He grabbed at her, yanking her to her

feet, the flimsy material of the negligée tearing beneath his hands with an ugly sound. He shook her like a terrier shaking a rat.

'The name, the name!' he shouted.

'Elli . . . stop . . . he . . . Shelley. His name is Shelley!' she screamed finally, pulling away from him, falling back on to the sofa, panting.

'Oh, my God,' he said. He stood there, swaying, perspiration speckling his forehead, his thick lips apart, loose. 'Oh, God.'

'Elli?' she said. 'What is it? *Leibchen*, what . . . ?'

'None of that,' he snapped. 'Enough of that!'

Theresa von Rodeck looked at him and the look on his face made her heart sink. Something had gone terribly wrong and she did not know what it was. She wanted to cry, cry from the frightened realisation that it had all gone wrong and it wasn't because she hadn't done exactly what Reinhard had said, something else had caused it, the man's name, and Elli's face was hard as stone and *Klaus had looked like that when she didn't do it right and then he would get the riding whip and* . . . Theresa von Rodeck shuddered, putting her arms tightly around herself, rocking her body slightly to and fro, whimpering to herself as Stewart paced the room, furiously, as if he was trying to contain an anger that was about to burst out of him. Jesus God, the American was thinking, Jesus God, that's the end of it. He'd seen the signals between Washington and Gross at Bad Tölz, knew now: Shelley wanted the information to get to Campion and he had given it to him. But he'd been getting information for four weeks and not done anything about it — maybe there was time to work something out.

All right, he thought.

One: there was no guarantee Shelley would act on this week's information any more than he'd acted on the information Theresa had given him during the last few weeks. Equally, there was no guarantee that he would not. Okay, let's suppose he does. Stewart thought. No way he can really get Campion (he had seen the bodyguard Charlie Gross had put on the General, and they were pros), so if he tries, they will take him. If they take him, then he'll tell them — eventually — that he got the information from Theresa. He looked at the girl hunched up on the sofa, her eyes dry, sobbing. And she'd tell them about me, he concluded.

Two: I could kill Theresa. He allowed the thought into his head without flinching. It was a possibility. He discarded it as quickly as he had thought it. Too many people at HQ knew about her, about this place.

Three: try to find Shelley myself, get him before the G2 people do. No, he thought. It's no damned use. I'm not a gangster. Even if I found him, it's odds on I couldn't kill him, any more than I could really kill Theresa.

He lit a cigarette. There really wasn't any choice at all, and in the long analysis, he was a soldier and he had a duty to do. He went to the telephone, looking at it a long time before lifting it and dialling.

'Get Major Gross to the phone, on the double,' he said to the operator.

'I know what time it is, soldier! This is Colonel Stewart.'

After a moment he heard Gross's sleepy voice.

'Gross,' he said. 'This is Stewart. I'm at Lerchenfeldstrasse 38, first-floor apartment. You what? You know about . . . well, I'll be damned. Okay, listen: get a squad of MPs over here fast. Yes, I'm with her now. I'll tell you why if you'll listen. The woman has been giving information about the General's movements to a man named Shelley . . . wait, dammit, I know, but I just found this out myself . . . for the last, hold on a minute . . .'

He turned to Theresa, who lifted empty eyes to look at him.

'How long?'

'Since the beginning of September,' she whispered.

'Since the beginning of September,' Stewart said into the phone. 'Yes, she got it from me. I know, Charlie, I know. Yes, I'll place myself under arrest until the MPs get here. No, don't worry, I won't do anything stupid. What? No, I don't think so. Wait.'

'Did Shelley give you a telephone number, an address, any way of contacting him?' he asked the girl. She shook her head, the long hair screening her swollen face.

'No, Charlie, nothing,' Stewart said into the phone. 'Okay. Okay, I'll be here when you come. How long? Okay.'

He put the phone down slowly, looking at it as though he had never seen one before.

'They'll be here in twenty minutes,' he said dully. There was no expression on his face. 'Go and get dressed.'

For a moment she did not move and then he took a step towards her and she saw the deep anger burning below and behind the eyes like fire under rock. She got up, edging back away from him.

'Elli . . . ' she said, putting out a hand as if to touch him.

'Get dressed,' he said, turning away, the fire in his eyes dying abruptly. He went across to the table and drank the cognac in the glass, pouring another half tumbler, gulping at it greedily. All gone to hell, he thought. All gone to hell. Ahead of him the long grey vista of interrogation, imprisonment, shame; courtmartial, dishonourable discharge, returned home with his record forever marred. He drank down the rest of the cognac in one gulp, turning to get a cigarette from his jacket pocket, and as he turned he saw the door opening. A man whom he had never seen before came in, and then his eyes fell on the pistol in the man's hand. He had just time to recognise it as a Walther P38, his mouth opening to speak, when the silenced gun coughed. The 9mm bullet left the gun with a muzzle velocity of 1,115 feet a second. It entered Stewart's head one inch to the right of the median line almost on a line with the septum. Striking the bone of the eye socket the bullet tore its way through the brain cavity, ranging upwards slightly and emerging just below the crown of the head, taking with it approximately four square inches of the cranium. Stewart's body reacted to the astonishing shock of the wound, his arms and legs jerking wildly into rigidity as the impact smashed him backwards against the wall, completely dead and not moving. The man in the doorway did not even look at the bloody slime on the wall above and behind where Stewart's body had fallen, but crossed the room on noiseless feet towards the bedroom door.

'Elli?' Theresa von Rodeck said. 'Was that you? What . . . ?'

She was bent over, wriggling into her dress as the man loomed in the doorway. Theresa looked up, a propitiating half-smile forming on her face. Her mouth fell open as the vocal cords tensed to scream, a hand coming up in a futile gesture of defence. Even as the sound formed in her throat the gun coughed again and the bullet slammed her backwards in a tangled mass of legs and arms, the top half of her face gone, blood matting the golden hair spread on the obscenely-dyed black sheets. She never even knew who had killed her.

26

Bad Tölz, Bavaria
30 September 1945

James Green was damnably, utterly, bone-achingly tired, despite the snatches of dream-haunted sleep he had been able to grab during the long, droning, interrupted flight. His eyes felt gritty and swollen, and his body sluggish, reluctant to obey the commands of his brain.

Charlie Gross met his airplane and drove him up through the pretty valley of the Isar, filling Green in on developments since his departure from the States — in particular the murder of Colonel Stewart.

'Seems pretty obvious that Shelley's ready to move, Jim,' Charlie Gross said. 'He's got the information he was waiting for, whatever it was. And so he had no further need for the Von Rodeck woman.'

'You think Stewart was . . .'

'The innocent bystander? Yes, I do. My

guess would be Shelley went to the apartment to kill von Rodeck. He found Stewart there. Maybe Stewart recognised him . . . he's on Stewart's lists of invitees for Campion's press junkets, although that doesn't mean a damned thing. Not that it matters. They're both good and dead.'

'How were they killed?'

'Shot through the head . . . oh, what weapon? About a 9mm, the Doc said. Probably a Walther.'

'And Campion's schedule? Can we change it?'

'All but one thing, Jim. He's got to go to Frankfurt on Thursday. To see Eisenhower. Scuttlebutt is that Ike's going to bust him.'

They swung around a corner, crossing a bridge, and the little town lay ahead of them, the onion dome of its church poking above the gabled roofs of the Marktstrasse. A few minutes later they were in Campion's walled and turreted headquarters. Once an SS training school. The General rose from his chair behind a cluttered desk to shake hands with the man from Washington.

He looked smaller, somehow, than Green had expected, although Campion was a tall man. Almost, he thought, as if Campion had shrunk inside himself. There was none of the flamboyance he had expected. The General was wearing an old Eisenhower jacket and ordinary GI trousers.

'Perhaps you other gentlemen would excuse us,' he said to his officers. 'I'd like to talk with Major Green in private.'

When the room was empty, Campion leaned back in his chair. The old eyes, tired but still shrewd, weighed Green carefully.

'Well, Major,' Campion said finally. 'You look about as bad as I feel.'

'Well, General,' Green replied. 'I hope not.'

Campion laughed, a short, barking sound.

'You know about me, of course. About this political stuff?'

'Sir?'

'Oh, come on, Major, don't fence with me. You've just come from Washington.

You're a special presidential envoy. What have you got to tell me?'

'Sir, I think you may be misunderstanding my reason for being here,' Green said. 'My job . . . '

'Is to soften me up for Eisenhower,' Campion snapped. 'All this bullshit about an assassination. Christ, man, if someone wanted to knock me off, he could do it fifty times a day, any day of the week — why would he go to all this trouble?'

'I wish I knew the answer to that question, General.' Green said, and the sincerity in his voice made Campion drop his head, glare at Green from beneath the jutting eyebrows.

'Damned if you don't make it sound like you mean it,' he said.

'I do, General, believe me.'

'And you haven't got any word from Truman for me?'

'No, sir.'

'Hm.' Campion got up and walked around the desk. He unscrewed the top of a thermos flask and poured some coffee, raising his eyebrows towards Green, who nodded. Campion brought the cup across and hitched his rump on the corner of his desk, frowning down at Green.

'We used to be such damned good friends, you see,' he said. He wasn't really talking to Green, the younger man decided, but just speaking his thoughts aloud. 'When Ike gave me Torch in 1942, we had the most marvellous relationship. But it all went to hell somewhere. That's a lesson for you, son. Speak your mind in this man's Army and they call it 'indiscretions.' Indiscretions, mistakes! It's always the goddamned paper soldiers telling the goddamned fighting men not to commit *indiscretions*!' His lips curled as they formed the word. 'Do you know I graduated from the Point two years before Eisenhower enrolled as a cadet? It's true. He was still in training at Tank Corps centre when I was getting my ass shot off in France. Not,' he hastened to add, 'that Ike's any the less of a soldier for that. No. Not at all. It's hard to explain how you feel about another man, isn't it? How can you almost love him as a brother, a friend, and then suddenly find he doesn't think the same way you do, feel the same way about things. You ever have that happen to you, Major?'

'Yes sir,' Green said. 'Once in a while.'

'Right,' Campion said. 'Now they say he's going to break me, take my command away. Did you know that?'

'Only what I heard on the grapevine, General.'

'Hah,' Campion said, slapping his thigh. 'Never fails, does it? The vultures always know where the meat is going to fall. And they've been waiting for this carcase a long, long time. Well, I fought my war to win it, not to win elections.'

'Sir, I don't think . . . ' Green began uneasily.

'Sit down, son,' Campion said. 'There's only the two of us in here.

'I won't tell tales on you, you don't tell tales on me, okay? If I say Eisenhower was out of his depth as Supreme Commander, it's only an opinion, isn't it? If I say the war was too much for his talents, it's only what I think, not necessarily the truth. Know-how, so-so; strategic and tactical planning, six out of ten; that's how I'd mark his term paper.

It seems goddamned funny to say that and know he's going to bust me, I'm going to be a nothing, a retired general. And he's going to go on to become President of the United States. Did you know that — did you know that was his ambition?'

'No, sir, I didn't.'

'Aaaah, it doesn't matter,' Campion said. 'I've known this was coming. It happened once before.'

'Sir?' Green said. He knew Campion's record inside out, and the General had been many things. But he had never been broken, retired.

'Sorry, son,' Campion said, smiling frostily. 'A quirk. I have a belief in reincarnation. It wouldn't interest you.'

Green made a protest, but Campion waved it aside.

'It's all right, son,' he said. 'Scares the bejeezus out of my own boys sometimes, and they're used to it.' He sighed. 'I'd have liked to see my wife again, just the same.'

'Aren't you going back to the States, General?'

'No, son,' Campion said. 'I don't believe I am.'

'Sir, if you're worried about the assassination threat, don't be — I'm confident we're going to pick Shelley up before he has a chance to make an attempt.'

'Not Shelley, not you, not anything, Major,' Campion said, getting off the corner of the desk and going back to sit in his own chair. 'Just something . . . ' His eyes cleared, as if he had come back into himself from somewhere else. His spine straightened and he fixed Green with a baleful eye. Green was startled by the change in the man.

'All right, Major,' Campion rasped. 'Let's get everyone in here and we'll listen to what you've got to say. *French*!'

Lieutenant Colonel French came into the room.

'Get 'em all in here, Jim,' Campion growled. 'They'll probably enjoy hearing how someone's going to kill me.'

'Yes, sir, General,' French grinned. Campion looked up sharply, but French was already at the door, beckoning the other officers to come into the room. Green nodded, shaking hands as each was introduced to him. Colonel Oscar Cook, Campion's intelligence officer, was a middle-aged, portly man with sharp eyes who Green knew had been an economist in peacetime. Lieutenant Colonel Jim French he already knew and liked, a big, tall, black-haired man with the build of a football player. Campion's Deputy Chief of Staff, Paul Harlow, was also a Lieutenant Colonel, also portly like Cook, but balding and older. The rest of the staff filed in, followed by a stenographer to take any notes that might be necessary.

'Gentlemen, you all know Major Green,' Campion said. 'I'll leave him to tell you himself why he's here.' He sat down in his chair and proceeded to write on the pile of papers in front of him, as if what was going on was of no concern to him whatsoever. Perhaps it isn't, at that, Green thought.

'Gentlemen,' he began, closing his mind to the scratching of Campion's pen. 'Although you may find what I am going to tell you difficult to accept, I want to impress upon you before I begin the extreme seriousness with which it is viewed by the President, the Chief of Staff, and the United States government. As of this moment, I want you to be in full readiness to co-operate with myself, and with Major Gross over there. Although all of you outrank us, in this business we are acting on the direct orders of the President. So if I give you an order, gentlemen,' he paused to let it sink in — 'I want it obeyed. Instantly, and without question. Is that clear?'

'That include me, Major?' growled Campion from behind him.

'You bet your ass it does, General,' grinned Green. Campion laughed out loud, and slapped his pen down.

'By God,' he said. 'I think I'll listen after all!'

And he listened as Green told them his story: of the hundreds of thousands of documents, dossiers, photographs and forms which had been checked, sifted, fined down to give them first thousands, then hundreds, then tens of possible suspects. He told them of their surprise at finding Peter Shelley on file, their excitement at discovering that Shelley's journalistic cover actually revealed he had been in the right places at the right times — Zürich and Munich especially vital links. He told them about Rafferty and the link with the Mafia, about his talk with Hinton in Naples, about the finding of the letter, about the details of the assassination, slowly, carefully explaining how it all tied together, why Stewart and the von Rodeck woman had been killed to break the link with Shelley, and how, although it ought to have nominally been a simple matter to pick Shelley up, he seemed to have disappeared off the face of the earth. He told them everything except one thing: that a senior SHAEF officer (whom many of them knew) was deeply involved in the plot. He had his own plans to bring that gentleman out into the open, and they did not include having him warned, however inadvertently, at this stage of the game.

He answered their questions for almost an hour, fending off some probingly accurate ones when he could, answering others in part where he had to. It did not seem likely that any man in this room could be a party to the plot, but he had no way yet of being sure. Until some other investigations he had set in motion could yield results, he was not about to show his hand.

'The fact that Shelley has made a move, killed his source of information about General Campion, indicates that he may be about to act. He knows the General is going to see the Supreme Commander in Frankfurt on Thursday. After that, he believes, General Campion will be heading for Speyer, near Mannheim, to do some hunting. We'll be changing those arrangements, of course.'

'Damned if you will, Major!' Campion snapped. 'I'm going. Been a long time since I did any shooting. Damned if you will.'

There was instant silence. Campion's staff waited, watching Green, wanting to see now whether he would take Campion head-on. Green pulled in his breath and turned around.

'General,' he said. 'I'll make a deal with you. If we manage to find Shelley before Thursday, you can go on your hunting trip. If we don't . . . I'm sorry, but it's off, and that's final.'

Campion glared at Green and Green returned his glare levelly. If he didn't face this one now, he'd have to face it later. Better now, he thought, hoping Campion wasn't going to force him to make the General eat crow in front of his whole staff. Maybe Campion read it in Green's eyes, maybe he was only trying him out, maybe the thought crossed his mind that he had plenty of troubles as it was, without taking on a special envoy from the President himself. Whatever, Campion shrugged and sat back in his chair.

'All right, Major,' he said. 'You've got a deal. But you'd better find this sonofabitch Shelley. I aim to go on that hunting trip, although I may just hold off long enough to hang the bastard before I leave.'

Everybody laughed, the tension going out of the room as Green turned back to face them.

'Right, gentlemen,' he said. 'With the General's permission . . . ' he paused long enough to draw a grin from the unrepentant Campion, 'I'm going to turn Bad Tölz into a headquarters, a nerve centre. I need to monopolise your Signals people for the next forty-eight hours.'

'My people will do everything they can, Major,' Campion said. 'Bill Gray there took over El Stewart's job. Bill, put your people at Major Green's disposal.'

'Yessir,' Gray said. He was one of the younger men in the room, Green noted gratefully. Wearing the insignia of a Lieutenant Colonel, Gray was about thirty-four, thirty-five, his blond hair closely crewcut, his uniform neat and correct. He looked efficient.

'We are going to put out a dragnet for friend Shelley,' Green said. 'The biggest dragnet we can get together. I want signals sent — take this all down, Sergeant,' he said to the stenographer, who hastily opened his book and started scribbling in shorthand, 'to every Command HQ in Germany, to all Military Police and Army CID offices, and to the

German civil police in all major cities and towns. A description of Shelley to be sent with instructions that if he is discovered, no action is to taken to apprehend him, but that we are to be advised immediately, while he is placed under constant surveillance. He's not to make a move without being followed. Every person he talks to is also to be watched. If at any time he is seen to be carrying a parcel, a package, anything that might hold a rifle or a pistol, we take no further chances, we freeze him off. But first we find him. No ifs or buts and ands. He is to be taken, and if possible — but only if possible — he is to be taken alive. And I want it all kept very, very quiet, gentlemen. Nothing in the newspapers, nothing on the radio, nothing that might scare him off. The major concentration of effort will of course be in the Frankfurt area — Frankfurt itself, Wiesbaden, Offenbach, Darmstadt, Mainz as far as Koblenz in the north, Trier in the west, Mannheim south, and Würzburg east. Intense effort in that area, but I don't mean by that our effort will be any less intense anywhere else. I want Shelley found, gentlemen — and so does General Campion. Although it seems we may have slightly different reasons.'

He looked at his watch, realising he hadn't reset it. It was still on Eastern time, showing 9 o'clock. They're just getting started there, he thought. And so are we here, came the next ironic reminder.

'Three pm,' he said. 'Let's get this show on the road. With the General's permission?'

Campion got up, a fierce expression on his face.

'You'd don't act like a man who needs my permission for anything, Major,' he growled, his face breaking into a smile. 'Except for one thing.'

'Sir?'

'You'll need my permission to dine with us in those clothes,' Campion said. 'And you have it. Seven o'clock, sharp. That's all, gentlemen!'

27

Frankfurt
1 October 1945

If you walk past the Hauptbahnhof in
Frankfurt today, heading towards the
Platz der Republik, you will find yourself
in the Dusseldorferstrasse, and because
they are building, as they seem to have
been building in Frankfurt for the last
thirty wears, all around the main station
(you'll see the derisory *100 Jahre
Baustelle* graffitti on the hoardings), you
will probably walk beneath the stone
arcade that ends on the corner of the
Mainzerstrasse. About halfway along, on
your right, there is an archway leading
through to the Niddastrasse, where trucks
pack the narrow street, unloading into the
offices and warehouses there — furriers
and wholesale dress merchants, Frankfurt's small equivalent of 7th Avenue at
34th, the garment centre. In 1945 this

lowering October day, the Niddastrasse and the area within a mile of it in any direction was a pile of ruins, rubble, broken rabbit warrens of brick and masonry in which, astonishingly, people made some kind of home. There were certain parts of Frankfurt that the Allied bombers had left alone, because someone at the top had decreed that after the conquest of Germany, Frankfurt would be the headquarters of the Allies. But those orders had naturally enough not included the complex of railway marshalling yards and passenger lines which spread out and behind the Hauptbahnhof. They had been cruelly, mercilessly, unsparingly wiped out by the droning bombers, the Americans by day and the British by night, and because bombing was then and is now an unscientific science, an inaccurate and indiscriminate weapon, everything within a mile of the station had been flattened, too. Yet still the people hung on to their interrupted lives — those who survived, or those who came after the raids had stopped, like the two men who crouched now over a shortwave transmitter in the basement of Niddastrasse 31, one transcribing furiously as the buzzing receiver broadcast its message.

When the buzzing stopped, he acknowledged the message quickly, his hand tapping out the coded signals fluently. He turned and passed the message to the second man, who nodded, and went to a table lit by two candles. Taking a small black book about the size of a pocket diary from his inside jacket pocket, the second man hunched over the paper, decoding the message.

'What does it say?' the first one said.

'*Moment, moment,*' the second growled. 'These blasted codes.'

He was quite old, nearing sixty; his clothes a shabby mixture of the kind you could see any day on the streets. Gray haired, his face lined and tired, he looked like a factory worker, perhaps, or some other kind of manual worker. His name was Manfred Eisenach and he was a senior agent of the Russian Intelligence apparat in West Germany. His colleague, the one who used the transmitter, was also a Russian agent. He was considerably younger than Eisenach, no more perhaps than forty, although it was hard to tell these days. He was tall, thin, his face sunken and gaunt. When he opened his mouth his gauntness was explained, for he was completely toothless. He had always had bad teeth, and the bad breath that went with them; and with dental treatment not only almost impossible to get, but also astronomically expensive when you could, he had simply had all his teeth removed. His name was Albert Müller.

'We are to put in hand immediately a search for a man. Peter Shelley. American journalist. Height, weight, eyes, hair, so. Believed in Frankfurt area. Must be found before — great Jesus, do they think we can work miracles on the money they give us?'

'Before Thursday 4 October midday latest,' Müller muttered, reading the message over Eisenach's shoulder. 'No expense to be spared, no time wasted. Extra funds will be provided through usual channels.'

He spat on the floor. 'How much, of course, they do not say. As usual.'

'When found, Shelley is to be placed under constant surveillance. All contacts and movements to be reported to this office,' Eisenach went on. 'Bavarian dolts! Don't they think we're capable of handling it ourselves, or something?'

'It says confirm immediately, Herr Eisenach,' Müller said, warily. He'd heard Eisenach's outbursts about the Bavarians before. If it hadn't been for that Bavarian madman Hitler, Germany wouldn't be in ruins now. And so on. He didn't care to hear it again. Tonight — if these instructions meant what he thought they meant — he'd be tramping the empty streets again, hiding in alleys, always watching for the American Military Police, scampering across the broken piles of rubble, using the well-worn routes by which all the Germans who resented the American curfews evaded the orders of the Occupation forces. He sighed.

'Yes, well, let's get started, then,' Eisenach said. He started scribbling out the message on the back of the piece of paper. Beneath it he wrote a second set of letters, a random code taken from the black book, which would be identified during the transmission by a single symbol. When he was finished, he read it over and nodded.

'All right,' he said. Müller crouched over the transmitter and started tapping out the message, muttering to himself as he read the letters out. Then he waited. After a moment, the receiver buzzed a few times, acknowledging receipt. Müller switched off, folding the lid of the suitcase down and locking it. As he did, Eisenach lifted the flat stone flag nearest to the door, beneath which was a hole lined with odd bits of timber and flattened tin. The suitcase slid neatly into its hiding place and they lowered the flagstone, scraping earth off the broken wall to fill up the gaps. In another few minutes they were in the ruined doorway of the building, furtively slipping out into the darkness, using the shadows under tumbled mountains of shattered brick to move unchallenged towards the Karl-strasse and then into the gaudy, shoddy light of the *Tanzbars* and brothels on Moselstrasse.

★ ★ ★

Not far away, two American officers also stared at a piece of paper. It lay on a desk in the I. G. Farben building in the centre of town and it was signed by Major James Green, Department of Justice.

'So,' Rogers said. 'They're on to him.'

'And from the look of it, they think he's here in Frankfurt,' Gilchriese said. 'Which doesn't give us a hell of a lot of time. We'll have to handle it ourselves.'

'In which case,' Rogers said, 'we'd better get started.'

★ ★ ★

Green left things at Bad Tölz in the hands of Campion's new Communications Officer, Lieutenant Colonel Bill Gray — very capable hands, as he had discovered. Gray had worked his men furiously from the moment they had left the General's office, and it had been a pleasure to see the way the machine worked. All plans were now made, all contingencies allowed for. Charlie Gross would fly to Frankfurt with Campion, plus three ex-OSS men he had chosen — ignoring Campion's remonstrations now as he had done ever since Green had put him onto the job of guarding the General — as bodyguard over and above the General's own staff, French and Cook and Harlow. Campion was to be closely guarded every minute he was in Frankfurt. He was to travel nowhere without escort, plus following armed guard. He was forbidden to use any open transport such as a jeep or halftrack, or to at any time open the windows of the car in which he was travelling. Traffic Control was alerted to his route in from Rhein-Main, and a half-hourly sweep of the road was to be made by armed MPs to move any parked car if empty, and to question its owner if he was in it. A pair of outriders would flank Campion's car the whole way in from the airport, and he would be taken up the steps of the Farben building inside a flying wedge of bodyguards and MPs who would make it difficult, if not almost impossible, for anyone to take a clear, sighted shot at him.

As for what would happen after Campion's interview with Eisenhower — well, if they still hadn't turned Shelley up by then, the same deal in reverse: back to the airport, back into the plane and back to Bad Tölz where, like it or not, Campion would stay put until Shelley was taken, or killed.

Green sat up front in the C-47, talking with the pilot, a youngster from Boise, Idaho, who'd been ferrying supplies in and out of Munich from Britain for the past seven or eight months. He was feeling rested, relaxed after a night's sleep that for the first time had not contained the dream in which he shot one identical Shelley after another, killing them time and time again until his arms grew weary and still they rose out of the mist and came at him. He knew Campion was behind him, and he knew if Shelley got past he would kill Campion, and so he shot Shelley again, and another one would come at him and then he would waken. I wonder if Jason felt like that, he thought. The pilot swung the plane into a banking turn. He could see the ribbon of the autobahn below cutting through the flat, dun green of the land, Frankfurt off to the right hidden in a haze, and then they were down, bumping twice, engines roaring as the pilot reversed the pitch of the props. A jeep was waiting as Green came down the ladder, and within half an hour he was waiting outside the office of the Supreme Commander, General Dwight D. Eisenhower. Captain Butcher, Eisenhower's naval aide, showed him in, and Eisenhower rose from behind his desk to shake hands, the famous grin widening in welcome.

'Major,' he said. 'You've come a far piece.'

'Yes, sir,' Green replied. 'And there's still a long way to go.'

Eisenhower nodded, his face growing serious. He made a signal to Butcher, who went out, quietly closing the door behind him. Eisenhower motioned to an armchair in front of his desk, and Green sat down as Ike went back to his own seat behind the meticulously tidy desk.

At six o'clock, some two hours or so later, Eisenhower got up and pulled the curtains, shutting out the darkening streets. He pressed the light-switch, flooding the room with brightness.

'It's hard to believe, Major,' he said, slowly. 'I find it hard to accept.'

'Worse than that, sir,' Green said. 'I have absolutely no legal proof at all.'

'Yet you still think . . . ?'

'I think I'd prefer to wait and see, sir,' Green said quickly. 'If I'm wrong, no harm is done. I've given a very special separate briefing to the Army intelligence people. They know what to do. I'm afraid the next part is the worst: we have to wait.'

Eisenhower smiled, briefly. 'I'm used to that, Major,' he said. 'Besides. I've got another unpleasant duty to perform when George Campion comes in on Thursday.'

'Yes, sir,' Green said.

'Did he say anything to you?'

'No, sir,' Green lied. 'We didn't discuss it.'

'I've got to do it, you know,' Eisenhower said. 'When we were fighting, it was different. I kept him on a couple of times when Washington was asking for his head on a plate. I told him once, years ago, that if we ever got into a war, I'd be his Jackson and he'd be my Lee. He said no, it would more likely be the other way around, and that's how it turned out. George just wasn't cut out for civilian life, for the delicacies of international situations. God knows, neither was I, but . . . well,' he got up, shaking off the thought like a dog shakes off water. 'I don't imagine you want to hear about my troubles, Major — you've got troubles enough of your own. As for what you've proposed, I am in complete agreement. I understand why you can't put your request in writing, and I respect your reasoning. If Harry Truman thinks you're OK, then that's good enough for me. Go ahead with your plan. I'll cover everything here, don't worry.'

'Thank you, General,' Green said. 'And I'm sorry . . . '

'Don't you be sorry!' Eisenhower said, and for a second, Green caught a glimpse of the stubborn determination in the man concealed behind that winning boyish smile. 'If what you say is true, I want it out in the open, cut out of us as if it were some kind of cancer — which it is. No, go ahead, Major. Let me know if there's anything further you want me to do.'

Green stood up and saluted. The die was cast. All he could do now was wait.

28

Frankfurt
3 October 1945

The Russian agents found Shelley first
for the simple reason that their people
were all civilians, all ordinary-looking
German-speaking men and women asking
innocuous questions about an American
visitor. They were answered readily and so
the Russian search moved more quickly.
The Americans were hampered by their
uniforms and their weapons. Germans
sidled away when they saw uniformed
men asking questions, a habit they had
cultivated for the last ten years. There was
no distinction in their minds between
Gestapo and American Army. Uniformed
men asking questions were always bad
news, and there were more than enough
people in Frankfurt as in every other
German city whose papers were not in
the best of order, who had no desire to be

asked questions about their background, or their history, or their reasons for being in whatever place the military found them.

So it was at something after five o'clock on the Wednesday afternoon that Eisenach and Müller learned where Shelley was, perhaps three hours before the same information reached Major James Green in his office in the Farben building. Shelley was staying in *Gasthof*, Zum Wilden Hirsch, on the Offenbacher Landstrasse in Sachsenhausen. According to their informant, a German woman working in the place as a *Putzfrau*, the American was making no attempt to conceal his presence.

Müller and Eisenach hurried there at once. Zum Wilden Hirsch was a small place, not much more these days than a lodging house, used by Allied servicemen on leave wanting to sample the old town delights of apple wine and *Gemütlichkeit* which the local people had started once more to provide — there being little difference in the faces once the drinking started, and the money being, if anything, slightly more useful these days than it had been, say, a year ago. Shelley was not hard to spot. He was sitting at one of the plank tables in the long, smoke-filled *Stübl*, drinking beer with two other men. Eisenach nodded and went out, back to the transmitter in the Niddastrasse. Müller slid into a corner table, watching the three men at the table across the room, nursing a beer and counting the slow minutes crawling across the face of the big clock on the wall. He was near enough to hear what they were talking about, and soon realised that the other two men were journalists: their talk was of the best places to get good food in Germany. Hating them for their money, their well-kept clothes, their talk of good times in places he, Müller would doubtless never see, he sipped the beer and waited.

Eisenach was back in an hour. He slipped into the chair beside Müller, ordering a beer for himself and another for his companion.

'It's all organised,' he said quietly, his lips hardly moving. 'There'll be a car outside in an hour. If he leaves, the car will follow. If not, we wait outside.'

'All night?'

'If necessary.'

'God in heaven,' Müller said, taking a swig from the stone mug. Eisenach said nothing. These youngsters were all the same. They had no idea what real hardship was. Müller should have tried being in this business a few years ago, when the streets were full of SS uniforms, Gestapo everywhere. He'd have had something to moan about then, by God.

* * *

Colonel Howard P. Davis, Army intelligence, was informed of Shelley's whereabouts shortly before eight o'clock, after a routine check by MPs who had been detailed to question every hotelkeeper and *Gasthof* proprietor in the city turned in a report by radio that the man was at Zum Wilden Hirsch in Sachsenhausen. Checking on a large-scale street map he saw that the *Gasthof* was on the corner of a narrow, S-shaped street going into the old quarter called Auf dem Muhlberg. There'd obviously been an old windmill up on top of the slope there at one time, hence the name. He made his dispositions, moving his men carefully into the area a half hour later, positioning them in buildings commanding the street, a jeep with a mounted machine-gun stationed in the darkness beneath the newly-rebuilt railway bridge crossing the wider street where it joined the Darmstadter Landstrasse, the main drag heading south to Darmstadt and north across the Obermainbrucke east of the cathedral. He then spoke briefly by radio to Green. 'Let the word out,' he said. Then, with the two other intelligence men dressed like himself in the uniform of privates in the Ninth Army, he went into the *Gasthof*, taking a table in the corner. They looked like any three American soldiers on leave, and nobody took any notice of them sitting there drinking their beer.

Davis and his men were wasting no time at all, though. They checked the faces of every man in the room, watching discreetly from beneath eyebrows, or when the chance presented itself to take a casual look around.

'Those two in the corner,' Davis said. 'They seem to be very interested in our man.'

'That's what I thought,' one of his men, Sergeant Michael Ervin, replied. 'Shall I check them out?'

'When they leave,' Davis said gently. 'Go take a leak and pass the word.'

Ervin nodded, getting up and going out through the wooden door, not even looking at Shelley's table. Yet he saw and heard everything that they did and said in the minute and a half it took him to cross the room. They were talking about whether or not to go over to Bad Kreuznach for the new wine festival. They had a road map on the table and were discussing the best route.

At ten o'clock, the landlord came into the *Stübl* and told them it was closing time. There was the usual chorus of groans, but the beefy German looked as if he might enjoy any argument the GIs might give him.

'Trink up,' he shouted. 'Trink up an coe hom.'

Shelley and his two friends finished their drinks and got up. The two men said goodnight to Shelley, who got his key from the landlord and headed for the stairs as the two Americans went out into the night. Davis nodded at Ervin, who went out after them, keeping a discreet distance behind. They were picked up very quietly about two hundred yards further up the street by a couple of MPs, who had them into the car and away before they could argue. Davis spoke quietly, urgently, to the beefy German behind the little counter in the hallway. Surprised, the man nodded, and Davis and Lieutenant Philip Rowan, the assistant who had remained with him throughout the evening, took the stairs silently, posting themselves at each end of the corridor in which Shelley's room was situated. The stairway light remained on. The rest of the place was soon in darkness, silent except for the quiet sounds of people in their rooms settling for the night. They could see the strip of light beneath the door of Shelley's room, number 12. After about half an hour the light went out. Davis looked at his watch. It was 11.45.

★   ★   ★

In the unlit street four men sat in a black Volkswagen with a Darmstadt registration plate. It was cold outside and the windows steamed up constantly. The man in the driving seat cursed silently from time to time, wiping the window with the sleeve of his overcoat to make a clear spot through which he could watch the doorway of the *Gasthof*.

'Poor Gerhard,' he said. 'He'll freeze watching the back door.'

'Let him freeze,' said Müller, unfeelingly. 'He's not the first to have to do it.'

He squirmed around until he got the pack of cigarettes out of his pocket and lit one. He inhaled deeply, and just as he did, a sharp rap on the window made him choke, coughing furiously. There was another sharp rap and he wound the window down. His eyes bulged as the snout of a M3 machine-gun was pushed under his nose.

'Okay, folks,' he heard an American voice say. 'Nice and quiet, now. Everybody out.'

The car doors were opened abruptly, and the men inside saw that there was a tight ring of uniformed men around it, all of them training the ugly 'grease guns' unerringly on them.

'*Was ist denn los?*' Eisenach said, loudly.

'Pipe down, buddy,' the Sergeant who had first spoken said. 'Just walk down the street, quiet as mice, and nobody'll get hurt. March!'

As he herded them quietly down the street, they saw another soldier pushing Gerhard Weiss, the man who had been guarding the rear of the *Gasthof*, none too gently with the snout of his machine-gun, shoving him towards the dark shape of an army car they could now see parked on the corner of the Darmstadter Landstrasse.

Müller began to curse, softly, persistently, his voice growing gradually louder.

He was still cursing as he was bundled into the car and driven away, followed by the Volkswagen, driven now by a young soldier in the threadbare clothes of a worker down on his luck. It was almost midnight. The street was silent again.

★   ★   ★

They came at one twenty, roaring up to the doorway of Zum Wilden Hirsch with lights blazing, squealing to a halt outside, leaving the motor of the jeep running as they bounded out and hammered on the door until the owner, sleepy-eyed and puzzled, pulled it open. He saw the two Military Policemen standing there, revolvers in their hands, and raised his arms immediately. They pushed him back into the hallway.

'You have a man here named Shelley!' one of them snapped in German. 'Which room?'

Across the street in the house they had commandeered, Green nodded.

'It's Rogers and Gilchriese,' he said. 'Let's go!'

'*Zwölf*,' the landlord was stammering. 'Twelve.'

'Stay here,' the taller MP snapped. They went up the stairs two at a time, coming into the corridor like lions, the thickset one turning to the right, the other left.

'Here!' Gilchriese said. Outside, Green's men were fanning across the street, silent as wraiths. He moved quietly towards the door of the *Gasthof*, ready. Gilchriese was already hammering on Shelley's door with the butt of his pistol. 'Shelley!' he shouted. 'Shelley!'

A door opened down the corridor, and Rogers turned, his pistol coming up. 'Get back into your room!' he yelled. 'Military Police!'

At that moment Colonel Davis made his move, perhaps half a minute too soon. Green was at the bottom of the stairs as Davis snapped on all the lights, the signal to bring the men in the street running into the hallway below. The two MPs turned, mouths clamping shut with astonishment, guns coming up instinctively.

'Don't do it, Rogers!' Davis yelled and came down the hall fast from his end. Rowan stepped into view at the other end, moving forward. Below, Green cursed, starting to run up knowing he was going to be too late.

Rogers kept his gun coming up and Davis could see the muzzle, as big as a cannon, and he knew that if Rogers fired it he was dead, it was a three-fifty-seven Magnum and it would blow him apart at this range but he had nowhere to go so he kept coming and jerked the trigger of his M3. His gun and the revolver in Rogers' hand went off simultaneously. At precisely the same instant Rowan opened up at a range of no more than two yards; and the man called Shelley pulled open his door. Rogers' single shot smashed Davis to one side, blood splattering on the wall as the terrifying blast of the .357 took the side of his head away. Gilchriese, standing in Shelley's doorway, was ripped in half by the burst of fire from Rowan's M3, his finger tightening convulsively on the trigger of his revolver, a twin of the one Rogers had used. At a range of two feet the bullet from a three-fifty-seven will kill an elephant stone flat dead. Gilchriese's dying shot lifted the slightly-built Shelley off his feet and slammed him back across the room as if he had been caught by a fast-moving truck, a hole the size of a man's fist in his chest.

All of it, the whole ghastly bloody butcher's slab of it, was effected in the time it had taken Green to run up fourteen stairs, and he came into the corridor, into the stink of cordite and sweat and blood, to see young Lieutenant Rowan standing there, staring aghast at the carnage around him.

'Move, man!' Green shouted, as the soldiers clattered up the stairs behind him. 'Ambulances, fast!'

He knelt down quickly beside Rogers, who looked up at him with sightless eyes. He was still alive, hanging there by a thread. Colonel Davis had stitched a neat row of five .45 calibre bullets into Rogers' chest in the same second in which Rogers had killed him. Green tried to keep his eyes off the awful mash of flesh and black blood pulsing beneath the ripped, burned

MP tunic. The man's lips were moving, and he bent his head to try to hear what Rogers was saying. He thought he caught the word *trust* but the effort had been too much for the broken body. Rogers stopped breathing as Green bent over him and then he was dead. Green got slowly to his feet. The soldiers were standing behind him, gawping at the bodies.

'All right, all right,' Green snapped. 'Get those people back in their rooms! Form a cordon. You, soldier, get to a radio and get help down here, fast!'

'Sir!' the GI yelped, and ran down the stairs.

'This one's still alive, sir,' the Sergeant who had gone into Shelley's room called softly. With a stifled curse at his own slow-wittedness, Green went into the bedroom. There was a macabre smear of bloody tissue on the wall at whose foot the curiously misshapen figure of Shelley lay. Green checked the pulse. It was faint, thin. Christ, when would that ambulance get here?

He looked around, not really seeing the blood, the awful smears on the walls, the broken bodies. He checked his watch: 1.30. The whole thing had happened in less than five minutes. If only Davis had waited another thirty seconds we would have had them all, he thought, bitterly. Thirty goddamned seconds. He straightened up as he heard the harsh par-pee-par-pee of the klaxon in the street outside; a few moments later the medics came in, eyes wide as they saw everything.

'In here,' Green said. 'And very, very gently, soldier.'

He stood and watched as they lifted Shelley on to the stretcher, the paper-white face twisting into a rictus of agony as they moved him. Then he followed them downstairs, every sinew in his body aching with disappointment.

Rowan was standing on the kerbside, with the landlord of Zum Wilden Hirsch gesticulating furiously, talking loudly in German. How dare they come to his beautiful house and kill each other? Who was going to explain to the guests, he wanted to know, who was going to pay for the ruined carpets, what right had they to come in here shooting guns, he was a law-abiding German citizen and he wanted . . . his voice tailed off slowly as he saw the look in Rowan's eyes. The young Lieutenant turned on him, body rigid with anger, eyes blazing.

'Listen, you fat tub of lard,' he said in faultless German. 'One of the best men I ever met was just killed in your stinking fleabag. If you don't shut your filthy mouth this second I promise you, as God is my witness, that I'll burn the fucking place down around your ears with you inside it! *Verstanden?*'

The German looked at Green, whose expression gave him no help at all. His face sour and bitter, he stepped back into his own hallway.

'Take it easy, Lieutenant,' Green said. 'You did the best you could.'

'Oh, sure,' Rowan said. The reaction was coming, he was just starting to tremble. 'Peachy.'

'Get yourself together, Lieutenant!' Green snapped, wishing he didn't have to treat the kid this way. 'Take over here.'

Rowan looked as if he had been

slapped. His face went white and he straightened up.

'Sir,' he said, saluting deliberately.

Green returned the salute and got into the ambulance, which roared off. He stayed close beside Shelley the whole way, head bent to hear anything the man said. When they got to the *Krankenhaus* Shelley was dead. Green got out of the ambulance like an old man and watched them carry the body inside.

'Dead, Jim?' It was Charlie Gross. He'd picked up the radio signals and come straight to the hospital.

'As a mackerel,' Green ground out. 'Never had a chance with that wound.'

'Did he say anything, anything at all?'

'Yeah, but it didn't make any sort of sense.'

'Try me.'

'He said. 'So that's why he wanted the cheque drawn to cash.''

'You're right,' Gross said. 'It doesn't make any damned sense at all.'

29

'Here he comes,' somebody said, and the correspondents all surged towards the doorway through which Campion was coming, photographers holding their cameras above the surging mob, men cursing as the hot flashbulbs touched exposed hands and faces, jostling, shouting, yelling for a comment as Campion came down the steps, a wedge of MPs in front of him pushing the reporters back.

Campion's face was pale and tense and he came to a halt like a cornered bull, the journalists bucking back in front against the pressure from behind.

'Get the hell back out of the goddamned way!' Campion yelled, his voice thin and high.

'Come on, General!' one of the reporters shouted. 'Did Ike bust you?'

Campion went deathly white, and for a moment the men in front of him cowered back, fearing he might strike one of them. They saw Campion make a great effort, getting control of himself.

'There will be an official communiqué at 1600 hours,' he snapped 'That's all I've got to say!'

There was a yell of disbelief, the journalists and photographers clamouring at the big man as he pushed the MPs aside and got into the passenger seat of the Mercedes standing at the kerbside in front of the main I. G. Farben building, its engine running.

'Get me the — get me away from here!' he yelled, and those nearest to the car saw a glint of tears in the pale eyes. They fell back as the automobile roared into movement, getting out of its way as the driver trod on the accelerator. With a shriek of burning rubber, the car jerked forward, the driver whamming off down the road towards the autobahn.

From his vantage point on the fourth floor, Major James Green watched the car until it disappeared into the distance. He touched his forehead in a sort of salute.

'Good hunting, General,' he said softly.

He had said his goodbyes to Campion much earlier in the day, before Campion's final interview with Eisenhower. He had the feeling that Campion was glad to have someone to talk to, to take his mind off what he knew was coming, and so he had told him about the events of the preceding night, and what had led up to them.

'You knew about Rogers?' Campion asked.

'Yes, sir,' Green replied. 'That was my ace in the hole. All the way through the investigations, right from the moment we found Rafferty's letter, Rogers' name was never mentioned. He was under surveillance of course, but he never put a foot wrong. What surprised us was that Gilchriese was involved too. We didn't know that.'

'You say you think they were mixed up in that business of the gold reserves disappearing?'

'There seems every reason to think so, although we don't yet know to what extent. At any rate it's a lead for army intelligence to follow up. There are a lot of gaps that need to be filled in, one way and another.'

Campion nodded. Like Green, he knew that although the Army moved slowly, it moved inexorably. The investigations would remain on file, the options open, until one day, somewhere, some time, they would stumble upon a link, a clue, a lead that would make all the other pieces fit.

'Well, son, you did a fine job,' Campion said.

'I guess so,' Green replied.

'You don't seem particularly happy about it,' Campion suggested, sensing something in Green's demeanour that hinted at dissatisfaction, something.

'I can't help feeling, just that seat-of-the-pants sort of feeling, that it's all too pat,' Green said, feeling for the words to express what he was trying to say. 'Shelley was supposed to be a top professional, who had worked several times for the Mafia. Yet he was a sitting duck at that *Gasthof*. The Russians were on to him as well as our people.'

'They wanted him for political purposes, I imagine.'

'That's right. Just think what they could have done to our image in Germany if they produced a man who had confessed to being hired by one of General Eisenhower's senior officers to assassinate you, sir.'

'Yeah,' Campion drawled. 'But there's all kinds of ways to bump off an old fogey like me, son. As you're about to witness.'

'Sir . . . ' Green began, but Campion held up a hand.

'No, let's don't talk about that,' he said. 'It'll come soon enough.

'I'm sixty-six-years of age, and I've done my best as God gave me the chance. And so have you son, whether you've left some loose ends or not.' He got up, making a production out of it, then thrust out his hand.

'I take it you're going to let me go on that hunting trip now,' he smiled.

'Yes, sir,' Green replied. 'I've even called off the bodyguard.'

'Goodbye, Major,' Campion said.

'Goodbye, General,' Green replied. He saluted as the old man went out of the room. It was noon. By one o'clock Eisenhower had taken the Ninth Army away from him, relieved of his Military Governorship, virtually retired Campion on the spot.

He turned back from the window. He had a hell of a lot of work to get done before he could return to the States. There would be briefings for army intelligence, for G2s from every command in Europe, for naval and airforce intelligence services, here and in America. There would be written reports (he groaned aloud at the thought of them) for NIA in Washington, for the President and his Chiefs of Staff, for SIS and SOE in England, a final drawing together of all the threads of a case which had had roots in three continents. Downstairs the interrogation of the agents who had been picked up in Sachsenhausen would go on until one or all of them broke, and that information, too, would be fed back to him to assess and act upon. He would have to go through every single file

Rogers and Gilchriese had ever opened at SHAEF, searching for any clue to their involvement both in the theft of the Reichsbank gold and the Shelley affair. He might get back to the States by Christmas, he thought, with a little luck. Maybe he would call on Jenny Davidson, tell her what had happened. No, no way: this thing would stay buried in the top secret files until one day it was broken. What the hell, he thought, I could call her anyway. Take her to a show; he remembered she was keen on musicals. Then the ghost came back. Shelley, he thought, you were too easy. *Why were you so easy?*

30

Mannheim
4 October 1945

The Mercedes rumbled across the shattered bridge, repaired by army sappers to take light traffic, moving at ten miles an hour. General Campion sat in the passenger seat up front, his face drawn and white. He hadn't spoken the whole time, not a word since they had roared out of Frankfurt and down Highway 38 towards Mannheim. In the back seat were Lieutenant Colonel French and Campion's deputy Chief of Staff, Lieutenant Colonel Paul Harlow. The driver was PFC Henry Forrest, a staff driver from SHAEF HQ who had been placed at Campion's disposal by Eisenhower for the trip down to Speyer, where the three men planned to do some hunting. The woods around the little 17th century town — which had miraculously escaped the bombing that destroyed its larger neighbour to the north — were rich in pheasant. They had all booked rooms at the Goldener Engel.

After a few attempts to get Campion talking, French and Harlow had given up, and sat now in the rear seats, watching the ruined town slide by as they crossed the Rhine, the late afternoon sun bright and crisp.

'Looks like it might brighten up, boys,' Campion said unexpectedly, coming out of his reverie. French and Harlow looked at each other and Harlow shrugged.

'Yes, sir, it does. Maybe we'll bag a few.'

'That quarter-tonner still with us?'

'Yes, sir, he's right behind,' Harlow said, squinching around in his seat.

'Good, good,' Campion said. 'No use our getting there if we don't have the guns.'

'Don't worry, General,' French said. 'He knows better than to keep you away from those birds.'

'He damned well better,' Campion growled, smiling mock-ferociously.

His eyes were on the ruins of

Ludwigshafen on their right as the young private manoeuvred the car between the trucks parked everywhere, heading for the road south.

'Look at that mess,' he said. 'Now I know what the man meant when he said war is hell.'

He sighed, as Private Forrest accelerated, leaning back against the seat, looking out through the open window.

'Maybe that's why I always loved it so much,' Campion said.

They were up to about forty-five now, and the road curved quite sharply ahead of them, the corner blind as Forrest tooled the big sedan around it, tyres squealing slightly, the car under perfect control. He was feeling pleased with his driving when he saw the truck. It was parked smack on the centre of the lane and not more than twenty yards in front of them.

'Christ!' he shouted, and jammed on the brake, the car sliding as the wheels locked, plenty of room to stop, he thought, it's all right, just —

At that moment the quarter-ton truck,

with Campion's equipment in it hit the car squarely in the rear, the driver standing on his brake but making only the slightest difference to the impact with which the heavy vehicle smashed into the car. The General's car jerked forward about twenty feet, slewing sideways slightly and hitting the rear of the parked truck, its hood jamming beneath the petrol tank of the higher vehicle.

And in the precise moment when the vehicles came finally to a crushing halt, as Harlow and French realised what had happened and clawed their way up off the floor, as Private Forrest turned his head anxiously towards his passengers, the man in the dense trees at the side of the road, the awkward-looking rifle notched firmly between two branches of a tree that formed a Y at shoulder height, pressed the trigger of the gun. It barked, rather than exploded, the hard sound flattened and dampened by the trees around it so that the men in the car did not hear the small explosion at all. He saw Campion's head jerk back and knew he would not have to fire again. He knew all about what the bullet he had fired would have done to Campion's spine.

In a rear-end collision at, say, 15 miles per hour, the human head — which normally weighs about 10 pounds — assumes in a split second an effective weight of 150 pounds. It is thrown backwards as though it were a 150-pound ball on the end of a very delicate chain — in the case of a human being, the chain being seven delicate vertebrae at the base of the skull. The weakest points in this chain are the points at which the top vertebrae join the skull, and where the seventh joins the eighth, which is part of the rigid structure of the shoulders. The maximum angle at which this delicate chain can be bent, and the maximum force which it will withstand, cannot be measured completely accurately, because every human being is constructed slightly differently. In this case, however, the victim was a sixty-six-year-old man whose neck had just suffered the equivalent force of a rear-end collision of twenty miles an hour immediately followed by a savage second blow which rocked his head back for the second time not just to the dangerous angle of sixty degrees which can cause severe injury and possible spinal damage, but to the fracture point of ninety degrees which will break the spinal cord of a healthy young man with every muscle braced against the shock.

'Jesus, sir!' gasped the young PFC. 'You all right, sir?'

'General.' French said, his voice more urgent. 'General?'

Campion lay slumped in his seat, head to the left, bleeding slightly from a contusion on his forehead, blood trickling down the side of his face from a scalp wound.

'Paul!' French shouted. 'Get to the truck! Get help! Move, damn you!'

Harlow looked at him, his mouth open in a wide O. Then he kicked the door of the car open and almost fell out, running back towards the driver of the truck who was coming towards the car, shouting, waving.

'Get out and see who the hell belongs to that truck, soldier!' French said, his voice under control now. He came around the side of the car and opened the door on the passenger side. It was crushed slightly from the collision but it opened easily enough, grating on its hinge slightly.

French unbuttoned Campion's Eisenhower jacket and felt for the heartbeat. With a savage wrench, using strength he did not even know he possessed, he yanked the driving mirror out of the roof frame and held it in front of the bloodless lips. There was no misting. Campion was quite dead, his neck broken.

The two men stood there until a unit of MPs arrived, and Campion's body was loaded on to a truck, to be taken to the military hospital at Heidelberg. The MPs took control of the scene of the accident, fencing it off with white tape and flashing lamps, waving on curious drivers in trucks and jeeps with imperious signals. They could find no driver for the truck, which later turned out to have been stolen and abandoned on this lonely stretch of road within a matter of four hours on that same day. The MPs got out their tapes and chalks and measured it all off, checking the stories of the two drivers against each other again and again and again until there was no question about it. It was an accident, a tragic, stupid accident that no one could have prevented, for which no one was to blame. They took their photographs, for the record, and then the vehicles were towed away. Nobody even noticed the piece of hard rubber, about the size of a .45 bullet, rolling around on the floor of the General's car.

★   ★   ★

They buried him in the American Military Cemetery at Hamm, alongside the thousands of Ninth Army men who had died in the war, near the grave of a young Second Lieutenant named Harold Sheridan who had been killed during the Ardennes offensive. Lieutenant-Colonel James Hansell French presented the Stars and Stripes which had draped the General's coffin to his widow. A twelve-man firing squad snapped to position, firing three volleys into the sky. When it was all over, Major James Green stood for a long time looking at the simple marker over the grave. *George Robinson Campion, Jr*, it read. *General, US Army. 1885-1945*. Much later, he left the cemetery, a lonely figure amongst the stark rows of white markers in the crisp green grass.

31

Zürich
8 October 1945

He sat in the Café Sprüngli, on the corner where the Bahnhofstrasse opens up into the Paradeplatz, a dark-haired man with pale blue eyes, perhaps thirty-five years old, sipping coffee. There was nothing special about him. No one in the place took any notice of him at all this fine October morning.

He lifted his coffee cup in a silent toast to Peter Shelley, late journalist of Munich, Germany; a slight smile touched his face as he thought of the grey men in government offices who would check and check and check again every single aspect of Shelley's life, in an attempt finally to close the file on him. They never would, he thought.

He had picked Shelley out the day after the first letter from Naples had arrived.

Shelley was roughly his own height and build, only the eyes a different colour. For two thousand American dollars Shelley had been happy to do the puzzling, but straightforward errands that were required of him, without tiresome questions. And so the man in the Café Sprüngli had met Rafferty as Shelley with his hair lightened slightly by bleach, coloured contact lenses made especially for him by a Zürich opthalmologist darkening his blue eyes. Then he had let Shelley pick up the briefcase from the locker in the Hauptbahnhof, Shelley open the numbered account with his American passport and the money in the case. He smiled. Shelley had even thought it a kindness when his eccentric employer had suggested it was perfectly in order for him to file some stories from Zürich for his paper. It was Shelley he had told to be in Munich or in Bad Tölz at the appropriate times, before he had sent him to a secluded chalet in Rottach-Egern, stipulating that Shelley should see no one, talk to no one until he left to be in Frankfurt by 2 October, calling at his apartment in the Agnesstrasse to let his landlady know he was going away on a trip first. And so Shelley, the obedient marionette, had danced happily down the road to his death, leading away the hounds that bayed at his heels without ever knowing they were there. The man in the cafe smiled again.

He had never really trusted the arrangements that had been made, trusting no one, making his own airtight arrangements, closing off all the doors as he passed through them. That business of the Frankfurt telephone number, its silly code, had been an obvious trap. And his instincts had proven right.

The woman von Rodeck and her unfortunate American paramour, he had killed purely as a precautionary measure. She had seen the real face of the assassin, and he had closed that door tightly. The old man in Madrid, old Don José, was dead; happy to be gone in the autumn of his seventy-fifth year, taking his memories of Vienna and Paris and the young man he knew as André to the grave with him. That door, too, was closed.

He smiled as the waitress poured him more coffee. He was many things, but André was not one of his names, nor France his country. The gun the old man had fashioned with such loving care was at the bottom of the Rhine, somewhere below the old wooden bridge which spans the river at Säckingen, the town through which he had entered Switzerland.

Yes, he thought, that door, too, is closed forever.

*   *   *

At the end, of course, he had realised there was no longer any need to kill Campion. He had the money — and fifty thousand was a tempting figure for having done nothing. He could have taken it and nobody the wiser, except for one thing — the people who had sent Rafferty. They knew that he was a professional and respected him. So in the end he had killed Campion out of pride. So that they would know he had done what he had been paid to do. Now, when they heard of Campion's death, no matter in what form the news came to them, they would know that it had been done and he had done it. They had a long memory, and $50,000 was nothing like enough to have them on your tail for the rest of your life. As it was, they might come to him again and, if the proposition was right, he might accept. An uneasy relationship, he thought, but at least I control it.

So he had stolen the truck in Mannheim, abandoning it on the road around the blind corner only minutes before Campion's entourage roared into sight. There had been plenty of time to set up the gun in the spot he had selected earlier that day, firmly notched in the tree for a perfect killing shot. Don José would have been gratified to know it had worked so well.

He got up and signalled to the waitress, who brought his check. Tipping her generously, he went out into the Bahnhofstrasse. It was a bright, clear day with a cold wind coming off the Zürichsee. The bunting and flags were gone now from the shop-fronts; the summer was over. He crossed the Paradeplatz as law-abidingly as any Swiss and ran lightly up the steps of the Schweizer Kreditverein building.

Inside, he asked a question at the information desk and was directed to one of the counters. He placed the cheque drawn to cash and signed by Peter Shelley on the metal turntable, and the clerk worked the lever. His eyes widened fractionally as he read the amount, and he asked if the Herr would mind waiting for a small moment. After perhaps two or three minutes, an older man came to the window.

'I am sorry to have kept you waiting,' he said apologetically in Swiss-German. 'You appreciate it is necessary to verify a cash cheque for such a large amount.'

'I understand perfectly,' the man at the window said. 'Please don't disturb yourself.'

'You speak Schweizer-Deutsch very well,' the clerk said. 'You are Italian, perhaps?'

The man outside smiled, but did not answer, and the clerk nodded, blinking his eyes rapidly behind steel-framed spectacles.

'Well, sir,' he said. 'How would you like the money? In which currency?'

'Swiss francs, I think,' the man said.

'Fifty thousand dollars in Swiss francs,' the clerk said. 'Very good, sir.'

They never ask questions about money in Switzerland.

THE END

We do hope that you have enjoyed reading this large print book.

Did you know that all of our titles are available for purchase?

We publish a wide range of high quality large print books including:

Romances, Mysteries, Classics
General Fiction
Non Fiction and Westerns

Special interest titles available in large print are:

The Little Oxford Dictionary
Music Book, Song Book
Hymn Book, Service Book

Also available from us courtesy of Oxford University Press:

Young Readers' Dictionary
(large print edition)
Young Readers' Thesaurus
(large print edition)

For further information or a free brochure, please contact us at:

Ulverscroft Large Print Books Ltd.,
The Green, Bradgate Road, Anstey,
Leicester, LE7 7FU, England.
Tel: (00 44) **0116 236 4325**
Fax: (00 44) **0116 234 0205**

Other titles in the
Linford Mystery Library:

A TIME FOR MURDER

John Glasby

Carlos Galecci, a top man in organized crime, has been murdered — and the manner of his death is extraordinary . . . He'd last been seen the previous night, entering his private vault, to which only he knew the combination. When he fails to emerge by the next morning, his staff have the metal door cut open — to discover Galecci dead with a knife in his back. Private detective Johnny Merak is hired to find the murderer and discover how the impossible crime was committed — but is soon under threat of death himself . . .

THE MASTER MUST DIE

John Russell Fearn

Gyron de London, a powerful industrialist of the year 2190, receives a letter warning him of his doom on the 30th March, three weeks hence. Despite his precautions — being sealed in a guarded, radiation-proof cube — he dies on the specified day, as forecast! When scientific investigator Adam Quirke is called to investigate, he discovers that de London had been the victim of a highly scientific murder — but who was the murderer, and how was this apparently impossible crime committed?

DR. MORELLE AND THE DRUMMER GIRL

Ernest Dudley

'Dear Mr. Drummer. Your Daughter Is Safe . . . If You Want Her Back Alive It Is Going To Cost You Money . . . Don't Call The Police . . . You Are Under Observation, So Don't Try Any Tricks.' A note is left in the girl's flat by her kidnapper. Her father, Harvey Drummer, turns to Dr. Morelle and Miss Frayle to help him secure his daughter's release. The case proves to be one of the most baffling and hazardous of the Doctor's career!

MONTENEGRIN GOLD

Brian Ball

Discovering his late father's war diaries, Charles Copley learns that he had been involved in counter-intelligence. When Charles is approached by an organisation trying to buy the diaries, he refuses. But he is viciously attacked — and then his son is murdered . . . Seeking revenge, he is joined by Maria Wright, daughter of his father's wartime friend. They are led on a journey to the mountains of Montenegro — and thirty years back in time in search of a lost treasure.

MOON BASE

E.C. Tubb

On the surface of the Moon the 'cold war' continues: world powers watch each other and wait . . . After a series of mysterious events, Britain's Moon Base personnel are visited by a Royal Commission. Among them is Felix Larsen, there to secretly probe the possibility of espionage. But he faces many inexplicable incidents . . . What are the strange messages emanating from the Base? Where are they from? And what is the fantastic thing that has been conceived in the research department?

DEAD FOR DANGER

Lorette Foley

When a young Dublin woman is mugged and afterwards stabbed, the police look in vain for the attacker. But 49 Organ Place, the seedy apartment house where she lived, holds the secret which links her fate with that of a desperate and hunted man ... Detective Inspector Moss Coen is baffled by the discovery of another body. But when all the tenants suffer a final, devastating and deadly attack, the Inspector must go all out to find a merciless killer.